Steeped in MURDER

A Tea & Sympathy Mystery

BOOK 6

J. NEW

The Yellow Cottage Vintage Mysteries in order:
The Yellow Cottage Mystery (Free)
An Accidental Murder
The Curse of Arundel Hall
A Clerical Error
The Riviera Affair
A Double Life

The Finch & Fischer Mysteries in order:
Decked in the Hall
Death at the Duck Pond
Battered to Death

Tea & Sympathy Mysteries in order:
Tea & Sympathy
A Deadly Solution
Tiffin & Tragedy
A Bitter Bouquet
A Frosty Combination
Steeped in Murder

Chapter One

SPRING WAS IN the air and there was hardly anywhere more beautiful than the old market town of Plumpton Mallet at this time of year. The trees and hedgerows were brimming with tightly woven buds, waiting for the warmth of the sun to unfurl and proudly display their newest attire. Seasonal flowers, having laid dormant all winter, were finally beginning to bloom, showing off their vibrancy in random splashes of colour along the riverside walks and beneath the trees in the parks. For Lilly Tweed, the season was also bringing an influx of new clients to her Tea Emporium in search of natural remedies for seasonal allergies.

"Yes, I highly recommend the Butterbur infusion, Miss Mulligan," Lilly said, boxing up the leaves.

"I do hope it works," the older woman said. She looked positively miserable and had come to Lilly at her wits' end looking for a miracle cure. While Lilly couldn't perform miracles, she could certainly help alleviate the symptoms. Miss Mulligan pulled a handkerchief from her pocket and wiped her watering eyes before noisily blowing her nose. Covering her mouth, she barked out a rasping cough before asking, "And you think this honey will help as well? I can't bear to think I'll have to deal with these allergies for weeks on end. They seem to get worse every year."

Lilly nodded. "I certainly do. The producer is a local woman, and the honey is straight from the hive so hasn't been heat treated. It's much better for you that way. Just add a teaspoon to your tea each morning and I'll guarantee you'll start to feel much better soon. And if you want something for the afternoon, which will also help, I'd recommend the ginger and lemon."

"But don't mix them," Stacey said with a smile.

Stacey was the young American girl Lilly had employed to work in her shop initially, but now she was not only the manager of the Tea Emporium but also of the Agony Aunt's Cafe, which Lilly owned in partnership with her former nemesis but now good friend, Abigail Douglas.

"Stacey is right, Miss Mulligan," Lilly said. "It's best to take them separately, and in the case of the Butterbur, just one cup in the morning will suffice. It's best not to overdo that particular tea."

"If it will help these allergies, then I'm happy to take whatever you recommend. You can add the ginger and lemon to my order, please. You know, Butterbur sounds familiar. I think I remember my mother using it when I was a young girl. Is it also known as something else?"

Lilly nodded. "Coltsfoot is another name commonly used."

"Yes, that's it. Now I remember. We used to live near an old abandoned railway track when I was a young girl, and my mother, sister and I used to walk along it most days. There was always Coltsfoot growing up the banks."

"That's right. It grows well in poor soil. It was dubbed Butterbur in the past because the large heart-shaped leaves were used to wrap butter."

"How interesting," Miss Mulligan said, once again wiping her streaming eyes. "I didn't know that. You're a veritable mine of useful information, Miss Tweed."

"Here you are," Stacey said, handing the woman the beautifully wrapped package and a jar of the local honey.

"Thank you, dear."

"Do let us know how you get on, Miss Mulligan," Lilly said. "I'm sure you'll feel better in no time."

"I will. And thank you for all your help. It's refreshing to get such personal and knowledgeable attention in a shop these days. Everyone always seems to be rushing about with no time to stop and chat. And I learned something new, which is always a good thing."

"Adding the honey to our inventory was an excellent idea of yours, Stacey," Lilly said as they watched Miss Mulligan leave, her items tucked safely in a little carpet bag.

"Thanks. I remembered a little shop back home that sold it as an allergy remedy. That's what gave me the idea."

Lilly glanced at the large clock on the wall and realised the cafe would be closing in an hour. She wanted to pop in and check how Abigail was doing before she left for the weekend.

"I'm going to go down to the cafe now, Stacey. Are you sure you're okay with looking after Earl for the next couple of days?"

Earl Grey was the official shop cat. A former stray who'd landed on his paws when Lilly had bought the premises. He'd wandered in one day almost at death's door and Lilly had immediately scooped him up and taken him to the vet. It had been a hard fight for him, but he'd had a strong will to live and with lots of TLC from both the vet and Lilly, he'd pulled through and now counted the shop as his home. With Stacey living in the flat upstairs, she made an ideal pet sitter and Earl was equally at home with her as he was at Lilly's cottage. So much so that he'd commandeered one half of Stacey's bed as his own.

"Of course, I love having him around. And I'm happy to close up for the day. You go down and see Abigail. And have fun on your trip! I can't wait for you to get back and tell me all about it."

"Thanks, Stacey. I appreciate it. And of course I will. I'm really looking forward to it." Lilly said, moving to the front window where Earl was asleep in his basket, and giving him a goodbye pet before leaving. Outside, she gave her shop one last glance before making her way down the market square to the cafe. She wouldn't be back until Monday.

*A*S LILLY STRODE down the street to the cafe, her heart was beating fast with excited anticipation. Tomorrow she was going on the secret Santa trip with her old friend Archie Brown. She'd been absolutely stunned when he'd handed her an envelope at the staff Christmas party, which contained two tickets, one for each of them, for a luxury steam train experience. She'd been even more surprised at the swift chaste kiss on her cheek and his furious blushing, followed by a hurried exit. But the thing which had astonished her the most was her physical response; the quickening of her pulse, the butterflies in the pit of her stomach and the realisation of mutual attraction, obviously laid dormant for so long.

Archie had been her friend and confidante for years, ever since they'd worked at the paper together. Once she'd left and first opened the Tea Emporium, they'd naturally seen less of one another, but tried to find time to meet up for a meal or a drink at least once a month. As it happened, with Archie being the town's senior investigative crime reporter and covering the murder cases which Lilly had inadvertently been drawn into, they'd seen quite a lot of one another in recent months. But when had their friendship matured into something more?

She'd thought about it quite a lot in the intervening weeks, but found she couldn't pinpoint an exact moment. It was something which had developed gradually and quite naturally. But one thing was certain, having been great friends for so long, they had an excellent foundation to work from. She decided not to try to analyse it further. It was a pointless exercise. She'd let it progress at its own pace and see what happened. She did find herself humming a jaunty tune while she walked down to the cafe though.

Inside, she found Abigail having an impromptu staff meeting, taking advantage of the empty cafe now it was almost closing time, so sat down to listen.

"Finally, we have a new range of lemonades to add to the menu. All homemade, natural, and using locally sourced fruit and herbs. Sizes are in half and one litre carafes, with freshly sliced lemon, homegrown mint leaves and some botanicals added. Recipes are next to the barista station. Any questions? No, well thank you all for your time and hard work today. I think we can start to close up."

Lilly smiled as Abigail approached. "Have you had a good day, Abigail?"

"It's been excellent, Lilly. Very busy with hardly a moment to myself. Just the way I like it. How about you?"

"Much the same. I've just popped in for the monthly sales figures."

Abigail laughed. "You know this could have waited until Monday, but as it happens, I do have them ready for you."

"You know me, Abigail. I just want to make sure we're heading in the right direction."

"Well, I think you'll be pleasantly surprised," her partner said, moving to the back office. She came back waving a folder. "I've printed off the monthly reports from when we opened, so we can compare. As you can see, sales have been increasing week on week, as have the profits. The tearoom has proved an extremely popular venue for celebrations and is actually booked up six weeks in advance now. The staff are excellent and very happy working here. In fact, would you believe I now have a waiting list of people wanting to join the team? All in all, I think we have a little goldmine here, Lilly."

"Gosh, Abigail, this is much better than I dared dream about," Lilly said, looking at the figures with a practiced eye. "Well done."

Abigail waved her comment away. "I'm loving every minute of it. Now, get yourself off. You've got an early train to catch, I believe? And you need to look your best."

"I do indeed. Thanks, Abigail."

"Are you excited about tomorrow?"

Lilly leaned in. "Between you and me, I'm as giddy as a teenager."

Abigail grinned. "Well, enjoy yourself. You've more than earned it."

LILLY LEFT THE shop with a spring in her step. There was no doubt she and Abigail had had a rocky start to their relationship, and that was putting it mildly. Yet, here they were, best of friends and business partners in a very successful cafe. Sometimes it seemed surreal. She turned the corner and walked to the car park situated behind the market square. Her bike was used as a display outside the Tea Emporium, so knowing she'd be away for a couple of days she'd driven in that morning.

She took a leisurely drive home, waving to various joggers, dog walkers and people she knew who had taken the opportunity to meet up with old friends outside, congregating on the pavements for a gossip now the weather was a little better.

Back at home, she quickly shoved the vegetables she'd prepared that morning in the oven for her dinner, and while it was cooking devoted a little time to choosing her outfit for the train trip.

More than once she found herself holding up a dress or a jacket to ask Earl what he thought. It was a tendency of hers to speak to the cat like he was a human. That's what became of living alone with only a feline for company, then remembered he was in the flat above the shop. She had absolutely no qualms about leaving him with Stacey; the girl doted on him as much as Lilly did. It was just the cottage seemed that bit emptier without him around.

Eventually, after half an hour of searching, she settled on a pair of straight leg, herringbone weave trousers in mid-grey with button detail. A crew neck cashmere sweater in deep plum, and teamed it with her favourite full-length coat. She'd found it at a vintage sale and although it was a little more pricey than her normal purchases, she couldn't resist it. It was a classic 1940s silhouette, softly tailored with defined shoulders and lengthening panelled skirt, in deep peacock green velvet. She'd accessorise it with her flat, dark grey suede ankle boots, and a green and plum silk scarf. Simple dark grey drop pearl earrings and a matching three-strand bracelet would complete the look.

She'd just finished hanging it all on the outside of the wardrobe door, including the plum coloured crossbody designer handbag she'd received as an unexpected Christmas gift from Lady Defoe, ready for the next day when the phone rang. It was Archie. Even though she was due to see him the next morning, she found herself ridiculously pleased that he'd rung.

"Hi, Archie."

"Excited for tomorrow?" he said without preamble.

"More than you know. I've always wanted to do a trip like this. It's such a treat, Archie, and I'm looking forward to spending the day with you. It's been a long time since we've done anything remotely like this. Are you looking forward to it?"

"Absolutely. It's high time we went on a jolly. So, what are you wearing?"

"I beg your pardon," Lilly said, laughing.

"Good grief, Tweed, get your mind out of the gutter," Archie said, laughing with her. "I meant tomorrow."

She gave him a quick rundown of her ensemble. "Why?" she could hear scratching in the background. "Are you writing this down, Archie?"

"Yes, and you'll see why tomorrow. So, I've been looking at the itinerary, full silver service breakfast on the train to start with, including bucks fizz. Followed by elevenses, and as many beverages as you like during the journey, all served by our very own waiter. We'll be in the lakes late morning. Lunch is served at a five-star hotel with an award-winning restaurant. Lots of places to shop and explore while we are there. Then, apparently, there's a writer's conference at the same hotel in the afternoon. Not sure if there's an admission fee, but I thought we might take a look if you're interested?"

"That sounds very novel, Archie," Lilly replied.

"Oh, blimey," Archie groaned, then chuckled. "Tell you what, I'll arrange a comedy stand-up for you on the train."

"Don't you dare, Archie Brown."

"You'll have a captive audience. They won't be able to get away if that's what you're worried about. How about after breakfast before elevenses?"

Lilly laughed. "All right, that's enough of that nonsense. I have to go and take my dinner out of the oven. I'll see you in the morning."

"Six-thirty sharp at the train station. Don't be late."

"I wouldn't dream of it. Don't worry, I'll be there. Good night, Archie."

As she dished up her food, Lilly thought about how interesting a writer's conference sounded. Not being a writer, she'd never attended one, but she knew it was something that would be extremely attractive to Archie. And considering that was the train's ultimate destination, there were bound to be some writers taking the journey with them. It looked as though the trip was going to be even more fun than she'd thought.

Chapter Two

THE NEXT DAY, Lilly got up at the crack of dawn and took her time getting ready. She rarely had the opportunity to dress up like this and wanted everything to be perfect. She and Archie had agreed to get taxis to the station, as judging from the itinerary there would be alcohol served with every meal and neither of them wanted to drive home on their return that evening. They had no intention of overdoing it, but by the same token, they wanted to make the most of the experience. At quarter past six, she was finally ready and just heading downstairs when she heard the beep of a horn. The taxi was exactly on time.

Archie was already waiting on the platform when she arrived and bounded over when he caught sight of her.

He took both her hands and gave her a twirl. "You look absolutely marvellous, Lilly," he said, kissing both her cheeks then standing back to admire her some more.

"So do you, Archie. Very stylish. And I love your waistcoat."

It was a deep plum and grey combination weave which matched her jumper perfectly. She loved that he'd taken the time to think about how they would look as a couple. It wasn't twee in the slightest, but just enough to show they were together. His shirt was a white button down and he wore a grey silk cravat. The jacket was a dapper blazer in a slick silver grey tone with a unique pinstripe and check combination and he'd chosen black wool trousers and plum suede derby shoes to complete the look.

They stood in silence, looking at one another with silly grins on their faces for a moment before they were interrupted by the sound of a train whistle. Then the clickety-clack of wheels and the puffing of steam reached their ears as The Lakes Express came around the corner and into view. Lilly clutched Archie's arm. A minute later, it pulled into the station with a final hiss and gust of steam, which rose up to swirl beneath the Victorian iron and glass arched roof. It was an incredible sight and both Lilly and Archie were dumbstruck momentarily before Archie turned to look at her and said, "Got your Hogwarts letter?" Lilly laughed. "Come on. Let's get this show on the road, shall we, Miss Tweed?"

*T*HE LOCOMOTIVE AND the carriages were painted in a deep heritage green with gold accents and a matching liveried attendant took the first-class tickets Archie handed him, punched them and returned them with a smile and a tip of his peaked hat.

"Welcome aboard The Lakes Express, Sir, Madam. I hope you enjoy your journey today. Your designated seat numbers are on your tickets and a member of staff will assist you momentarily."

They both thanked him and stepped up onto the train, taking a right turn into the carriage.

"Oh, Archie," Lilly breathed. "This is incredible. It's like stepping back in time."

"I must admit, I feel like a film extra in a high budget murder mystery," Archie whispered back.

"Don't even think it, Archie. I don't want to jinx this trip before we've even started."

The interior was panelled in deep honeyed wood, buffed to a soft shine. Art deco ceiling lights ran the length of the ceiling, with matching tiffany-style lamps on every table. The plush carpet was a deep green, as were the curtains, and the plush high back armchair style seats were upholstered in deep green damask with a mink coloured ornate paisley design.

"Here we are," Archie said, indicating a table for four in the middle of the carriage. "We're seated opposite one another, next to the window."

"It's perfect, Archie. I can't thank you enough for such a wonderful gift."

As the carriage filled up, they were joined at their table by a large, handsome, well-dressed man carrying a briefcase and a well-worn book. Lilly estimated him to be in his early forties. Taking a seat next to Lilly, he shook both their hands and introduced himself.

"Vincent Wales."

"I'm Archie Brown, and this vision of loveliness is Lilly Tweed."

Lilly rolled her eyes, but couldn't help the grin spreading across her face.

"A pleasure to meet you both," Vincent said, tucking the briefcase under his seat and resting the book next to his plate.

The novel was clearly well loved. Its creased spine told of multiple reads, and there were yellow post-it notes sticking out in all directions. "Murder on the Orient Express," Lilly said, impressed with his choice. "It's one of my favourite Agatha Christie novels. It looks as though you've read it a time or two as well," she added, as the waiter served them a tall glass of Bucks Fizz each and the train began to chug slowly out of Plumpton Mallet station.

He beamed at her. "I'd say so. I'm on my way to the writer's conference. I'm working on a murder mystery and in order to do that, you need to study the best."

"I agree," Archie said. "Although I can't help but note the irony of reading such a novel while aboard a steam locomotive."

Vincent laughed. "Yes, you're right. Although it's a complete coincidence. Luckily, it's not the 1930s and I don't believe we have a former member of the mob here with us, so we should be safe."

"I assume it takes place on a train?" A woman's voice said from the seat behind Archie.

Vincent leaned into the aisle where the woman had turned and was looking at him, obviously interested in their conversation.

"Katherine Harp, I might have known," he said with a slight sneer. "I suppose it makes sense that you'd be unaware of such an acclaimed novel."

Lilly glanced at Archie and raised an eyebrow. He gave an almost imperceptible shrug in return.

The busty red headed woman pursed her lips and a second later was standing next to them. Hands, with their perfectly manicured talons coated in bright red polish, on her wide hips. She was a stunning looking woman in her mid thirties, Lilly guessed, wearing a tight black skirt, black and white polka dot top and a wide red belt cinching her waist. The ensemble was finished with black tights and black patent leather heels with a red buckle.

"And just what do you mean by that, Vincent Wales?"

"Now, don't get all defensive, Katherine. All I meant was with your preferred genre in makes sense."

"What, that I wouldn't read a classic?"

"Well, you hardly write classics, do you?"

"Oh, so you're a writer too?" Lilly said pleasantly, hoping to break the growing animosity between the two writers.

The woman turned to Lilly, a slight smile forming on her crimson lips.

"Yes, I am, as a matter of fact. But unlike this wannabe novelist," she said, waving a hand in Vincent's direction, "I actually have a number of very popular published works and am considered one of the best in my field."

"She writes smut," Vincent said.

"How dare you!" Katherine spat. "My romance novels are not smut. You're just jealous because it's unlikely your attempts will ever see the light of day."

"Au contraire, my dear, Katherine," Vincent replied smugly, tapping his briefcase knowingly. "My latest has netted considerable interest from the big publishers, I'll have you know. Some of whom will be at the conference later." He held up the Christie novel and looked at Lilly and Archie. "Who knows, perhaps someone will be sitting on a train reading my work for research one day?"

"I seriously doubt that," Katherine scoffed, about to walk away, but then suddenly changed her mind as she saw someone she knew. "Bobby Smith!" she exclaimed in excitement, darting past Lilly and Vincent in the opposite direction to her designated seat.

The name was obviously familiar to Vincent Wales, who muttered "Bathroom," before hurrying to the opposing end of the carriage, and to a WC much further away than the one in the direction of Katherine and her old friend.

"Well, isn't this turning into an interesting trip already?" Archie said, as the waiter brought their breakfasts. A full English to begin with, accompanied by tea or coffee, then croissants or toast with a choice of several honey's and jams. "Our table guest is a little rude, don't you think?" he continued, placing the napkin on his knee and tucking into the delicious spread before them.

"A little," Lilly said, peering over the back of her seat to where Katherine was talking animatedly with Bobby Smith at the other side of the carriage door. "I wonder if he's a writer too?"

"I wouldn't be surprised," Archie said. "Although I do hope they aren't all going to be at each other's throats the whole journey. In fact, I'd be quite happy if that Vincent chap doesn't come back."

Lilly laughed. "Oh, Archie, don't tell me you're not finding this just a little entertaining?"

Archie grinned. "Yes, all right, I'll admit to that, providing it doesn't get nasty. But I had hoped to have you all to myself. Oh, don't look now, but we're about to get company again."

Katherine once again appeared at Lilly's side, but this time, she had Bobby Smith in tow.

"Oh, drat! Where did Vincent go? I was hoping to reintroduce an old friend of ours."

"Hello," Lilly said, nodding at the older, swarthy looking man. "I'm Lilly Tweed and this is Archie Brown," she continued, as it became apparent Katherine wasn't intending to introduce them.

"So, how do you know Vincent?" he asked.

"We don't," Archie replied. "His assigned seat just happened to be at our table."

"Are you a writer too?" Lilly asked.

"No," he replied abruptly and turned back to Katherine. "Kathy, I'm going back to the bar. I'll track Vincent down later."

"If you must," Katherine sighed, watching his retreating back before turning back to Lilly and Archie.

"Gosh," said Lilly, glancing at her watch. "Is the bar open at this time of the morning?"

Katherine shrugged. "So, what is it that you two write, then?"

"Oh, we didn't know about the conference when Archie booked the trip. Although it does sound interesting. We're not novelists. Archie is an investigative reporter with the newspaper and I'm a former Agony Aunt at the same place. I run a tea shop now, though."

"An Agony Aunt!" Katherine exclaimed, clasping her hands together. "I think you just gave me a wonderful idea for a story. I've been trying to come up with a new protagonist for my next romance novel and I think an Agony Aunt would be a fun character to play around with. Can you imagine a woman writing advice for others but unable to find her own soul mate? Ooh la la. Tragic romance! Yes!"

Lilly cringed a little but gamely said, "Well, you're the professional. I'm sure you'll make it work."

"I must get these ideas down before I lose them. It was a pleasure," Katherine said, before scurrying back to her seat.

Archie turned to Lilly with a highly amused look on his face.

"Don't say a word," Lilly said, trying not to laugh.

"Ooh la la," Archie mouthed over his orange juice and the two of them started to giggle like naughty children at the back of the class.

"I WONDER WHERE VINCENT got to," Lilly said, as they finished their food. "Do you think he's all right?"

"I'm sure he is. Probably found a writer friend further down the train to talk to. Perhaps he'll stay there?"

"His briefcase and book are still here, Archie. He'll be coming back. Oh, here he is now."

There was a slight anxiousness to Vincent's demeanor when he returned, and he continued to glance about him as he took his chair next to Lilly. As soon as he was seated, the waiter appeared and served him breakfast, bringing fresh pots of coffee and tea for the three of them.

"Now, this is what I call a breakfast," he said, tucking in as though he'd not eaten for weeks, although Lilly noticed he still glanced around him at every opportunity.

"There's really no better way to travel than by train," Archie said. "Just look at this spectacular scenery. You really do miss so much by being in a car."

"It's breathtaking," Lilly said in agreement, taking in the lush green valleys and undulating hills, interspersed with craggy rocks and patches of woodland, all beneath a Periwinkle sky. "And we're so lucky the weather is fine. You can see for miles."

"Look, can you see the buzzard hovering over there, Lilly? No doubt got an eye on his own breakfast. Oh, there he goes!"

They both watched as the bird of prey dived, wings flat, and a moment later was airborne again, the quarry clutched in his talons.

Lilly, Archie and Vincent spent the next couple of hours chatting amiably and remarking upon the incredible views from the carriage windows. One minute they were looking at quaint little villages nestled in the valleys, the spires of the churches reaching up towards the vast expanse of sky, and the next, a patchwork of fields dotted with little white sheep or black and white cows that looked no bigger than children's toys, with majestic lilac grey mountains in the distance.

By the time elevenses came round, Lilly was astonished to find she was hungry, and tucked into a fruit scone served with cream and jam with gusto. Served, of course, with a pot of the finest English tea. Proper leaves and not tea bags Lilly was pleased to note.

"So, tell us about this hotel where we'll be having lunch, Vincent. Have you been before?" Archie asked, daubing a cherry scone with butter.

"Numerous times. The writer's conference has been held there annually for the last several years, although I've never stayed there overnight. The restaurant is an award winner, and the food is excellent. The hotel itself was built as a family home by some rich chap in the 1700s, I think, so it's full of little quirky areas. Now, it's a family run business with spas, hot-tubs, swimming pool and all that sort of stuff. There's cycling and walking trails through the estate and more formal gardens. And of course, fishing or boating on the lake."

"It sounds huge," Lilly said.

Vincent nodded. "About a hundred acres give or take, which includes a large wood and a herd of wild deer living nearby."

"I can't wait. Do we go straight there, Archie? What does the itinerary say?"

Archie reached into his inside jacket pocket and brought forth a printed sheet.

"We arrive at the station in," he glanced at his watch. "About forty minutes. From there it's a ten-minute stroll to the town for a meander and a spot of shopping for a couple of hours. Then back to the station where a minibus will pick us up to transfer us to the hotel for a three course lunch. Then we have a choice to either return to the town for the afternoon, explore the hotel grounds, or see if we can join the writer's conference. The day is yours, Miss Tweed. I'll go along with whatever you prefer. Once that's all done and dusted, we get back on the train to enjoy dinner and drinks on the journey home."

Lilly grinned. "It sounds wonderful, Archie, and I'm more than happy to attend the writer's conference. I'll leave that part to you."

The remaining time on the train sped by almost as fast as the locomotive itself and before long, they were stepping out onto a quaint little platform that looked as though it hadn't changed since the end of the Second World War. Painted in clotted cream and deep red colours, the ticket office was adorned with spring hanging baskets, old-fashioned lamps and surrounded by displays of stacked 1940s luggage, milk churns filled with more flowers and old fire buckets in bright red. The whole atmosphere was one of nostalgia and Lilly loved it, reminding her as it did of the film The Railway Children.

They said goodbye to Vincent, who was heading to the hotel straightaway, then entered through the ticket office archway and through the other side to begin the walk down a shallow cobbled lane to the small market town.

Chapter Three

THE TOWN WAS not unlike Plumpton Mallet with its cobbled square and array of both high street favourites and independent retailers, but it was spread out over a much larger area.

Archie grabbed a town map from a nearby stationery store and they discovered there were several old-fashioned yards, sites of former inns, stable blocks and remnants of the wool trade the town had been known for, now turned into shopping centres and arcades.

There were museums and art galleries, a beautiful parish church, numerous pubs and cafes and even the ruin of a castle with its heritage centre. And dotted all around were well established trees in all their pink and white blossom finery.

"I didn't realise there was so much here, Archie," Lilly said in awe. "We'll never have enough time to see it all."

"Well, in that case, we'll just have to come back another time, won't we? Perhaps for a long weekend?"

Lilly smiled. "That sounds like a wonderful idea. Where do you want to start today?"

"How about the Cultural Quarter?" He said, pointing to a section of the map. "It sounds very interesting. Quirky antique shops, art shops and galleries, plus lots of artisan establishments."

Lilly nodded. It sounded right up her street.

They explored happily for a while, entering nearly all the shops and picking up a few small pieces they could take home, then moved onto an enchanting little shopping arcade called The Shambles, with cobbled streets and tiny independent Tudoresque shops you stepped down into, selling everything from wool tapestries to handmade shoes. In a small jewellery shop, Archie purchased something Lilly didn't see, then promptly gave her a gift-wrapped box once they were outside.

"What on earth is this, Archie?"

"Just a little something to remember the trip. I thought it was you as soon as I saw it."

Lilly undid the cobalt blue bow and lifted the lid. Inside was a pair of gold and cloisonné earrings in the shape of a teacup and saucer.

"Oh, Archie, they're beautiful. I love them. Thank you so much."

She gave him a kiss on the cheek, and then told him to wait while she dashed back up to a shop she'd seen earlier. There was a perfect gift for him in the window.

Five minutes later, she returned and gave him a large box and waited with anticipation for him to open it.

The moment he unwrapped the tissue paper inside, he gave a loud laugh, put his arm around her shoulder, hugged her tight, and kissed her temple.

"Do you know, I saw this and was seriously contemplating going back and getting it. It couldn't be more perfect, Lilly. Thank you."

It was a tapestry waistcoat in deep blue with a quill and ink pot design embroidered in gold thread.

"I'm so glad you like it, Archie. It really is very you."

Their final stop was a bookshop which looked like it came straight from the pages of a Dickens novel.

"You should do a book on teas," Archie whispered as they perused the shelves. "I bet your regular customers would snap it up."

"Now there's an idea!" Lilly whispered back. "I could include some history, the differences between high and low tea, recipes and remedies. A bit about the shop and the cafe. I could even include my cocktail recipes. Thanks for the idea. I'll have a chat with Stacey about some research when we get back."

"Well, let me know if I can help. It would be lovely to write about something other than crime for a change. Now, I think we need to make our way back to the train station. The bus will be there shortly to take us to the hotel for lunch.

As they walked, Archie once more put his arm around her shoulder and Lilly put hers around his waist. It was the most natural thing in the world and Lilly wondered how she'd not realised before how perfectly matched they were.

WAITING IN THE station car park was a wondrous sight as they reached the top of the cobbled slope up from the town. Lilly was a big fan of vintage and there was nothing more vintage than a 1940s charabanc painted in soft cream and burgundy.

"I say!" Archie said, wandering around the old bus. "A 1949 Bedford if I'm not mistaken. And it's absolutely pristine. What wonderful work they've done to restore it. It looks as though it has just rolled out of the factory an hour ago."

Inside the seats were red and cream leather and despite their diminutive size, were remarkably comfortable.

"Archie, wouldn't it be wonderful to have something like this for the shop and cafe? It could be fitted out so I could provide afternoon teas and catering for events. Perhaps string some bunting across the front and a serving hatch. I could do events anywhere then."

"Now that's a marvellous idea, Lilly. I'll keep my eye out for you. Depending on what we can find and what condition it's in, would govern how much work would be needed. But I just so happen to know a chap who could do it."

"Really?" Lilly said, glowing with warmth at Archie's use of the word 'we.' "Let's do some research once we get home."

All twenty-nine of the charabanc's seats were taken, but Lilly recognised none of the other occupants. It was likely they'd taken the same train as them, but they'd been in other carriages. The writers they had met, no doubt, had gone straight to the conference.

It only took ten minutes to the hotel, where they were driven right up to the double width front doors and greeted by a butler in full uniform who welcomed them, then handed them over to a footman who proceeded to take them through to the large dining room.

It was immediately apparent this had originally been the family library. The floor to ceiling shelves on three of the walls were still in place and filled with books. In the centre was a huge fireplace, dormant now due to the better weather, hewn from a single block of stone. The chimney breast was a fancy, and no doubt pricey, Italian marble in browns and creams, with an oil painting in the centre depicting the original owner of the house according to the brass plaque below.

Double wide oak floorboards, obviously original, were scattered with Turkish rugs and the chairs, neatly tucked under damask clothed dining tables, were covered in crimson leather.

A waitress in a black-and-white uniform with a frilly apron showed them to a table for four in one of the bay windows, and once again they took seats opposite one another.

"I didn't realise the house was built so close to the lake shore," Lilly said, gazing out of the window in wonderment.

"Makes for one heck of a fantastic view, doesn't it? Maybe we should take one of those rowing boats out later?"

"Oh, yes! I love messing about in boats."

"Do you really? I love finding out new things about you, Lilly. And how much we have in common. I love boating as well."

Lilly smiled and reached across to squeeze his hand.

A moment later, the footman escorted another couple to their table to join them. Both were smartly dressed, he was in a deep blue blazer with nautical gold buttons, and she was wearing a long floral print dress, with her brunette hair in a matching scrunchie.

"Colin Kimble," the man said. "And this is my wife, Deborah."

With introductions made, drinks and meals ordered, Lilly asked if they were here for the writer's convention?

"Oh, no, not really," Colin said. "I'm not much of a reader let-alone a writer, and Deborah rarely has enough free time to pick up a book. No, we're here to look at property mainly. We're thinking of moving up here. Deborah wants to open up a shop."

"Where are you living now?" Archie said, taking a spoon-ful of wild mushroom soup with crispy croutons and chives.

"A medium sized village on the outskirts of Lincoln," Deborah replied. "We have businesses in the city, but I'm looking for a slower pace of life. We caught the early train yesterday and stayed in Plumpton Mallet overnight, then caught the steam train here today. Have either of you been to Plumpton Mallet? It's got the most fabulous new cafe with a tea room in the market square. A friend told me about it and I just had to see it for myself. Do you know it?"

Both Lilly and Archie grinned widely. "I know it very well," Lilly said. "I own it with a business partner, as well as The Tea Emporium, a few doors further up."

"Oh, that's brilliant. You've done such a great job with it. I adore the Art deco look. We'll definitely be paying another visit."

The four of them ate the exquisite lunch while chatting about light hearted subjects, then the Kimble's left citing afternoon appointments, while Lilly and Archie went in search of the venue for the writer's conference.

"Look, there's a sign here which says it's being held in the Chinese room," Archie said. "Just down this corridor, I think."

Not far down the hall, they found a tall thin man wearing horn-rimmed glasses collecting tickets and checking names on a clip board.

"Welcome. Do you have your tickets handy?"

"Actually, we didn't book but would love to attend. Can we pay on the door as it were?" Archie asked.

The man shook his head. "I'm sorry, I'm afraid not. We're booked to capacity. But if you want to attend the next one, this gives all the details, including the website," he said, handing him a colourful flyer along with a free book mark.

Archie thanked him, pocketed the information, and he and Lilly returned to the rear entrance and out into the garden.

"That's a shame. Are you disappointed, Archie?"

"Good heavens no. It was a spur-of-the-moment idea, that's all. Besides, it gives us more time for a bit of boating. What do you say?"

"Lead on, Captain," Lilly laughed. "I'm looking forward to it."

"OH, ARCHIE, THAT was great fun," Lilly said, as they boarded the train for the return journey. "Sorry you got so wet. I seem to remember rowing a boat being a lot easier in my youth."

"Well, thank goodness for health and safety. At least we were given waterproofs and a life jacket each; otherwise I'd have been soaked all the way through. And honestly, I didn't mind going around in circles for the first ten minutes, although I was beginning to get a little dizzy."

Archie laughed. "Next time you can row and I'll sit in the prow and give useless advice."

Lilly giggled. "It's a deal. Now, I think a drink is in order to warm ourselves up."

They took their seats and a moment later, their waiter arrived.

"Good evening, my name is Charlie and I'll be your personal waiter for the return journey. What can I get you both?"

"Something to warm us up."

"How about a hot toddy? We have either a classic or our own signature steam recipe."

"I'll have the signature steam," Archie said, looking at Lilly. "How about you?"

"Oh, definitely the same, please, Charlie."

Several moments after their drinks arrived, Lilly glanced up and saw Vincent boarding. She assumed he would once again join them for dinner, but he walked right past with his head down and almost entirely obscured by a wide-brimmed hat, sunglasses and his coat collar raised.

"Vincent?" Lilly said, but he ignored her completely.

"That was strange," Archie said as they watched him leave the carriage at the far end.

"Wasn't it? Mind you, he acted oddly this morning when that Bobby Smith appeared. Do you think he's trying to avoid him?"

"Looks that way. Perhaps he owes him money or something?"

"Mmm," Lilly said, thoughtfully. "Maybe."

Ten minutes later, with the carriages now full of happy passengers and stacked to the gills with shopping bags, the train began to chug its way out of the station with a shrill whistle and the customary hiss of steam. Then Charlie arrived with a tray of canapés.

"Gosh, these look amazing," Lilly said. "Can you tell us what they are?"

"Certainly, madam," he replied, pointing to each one in turn. "Here we have elderflower jelly with beetroot relish and goat's cheese on a caraway tuile. Port and Stilton toast here. These are gratinated pine nut and basil chicken with saffron mayonnaise. And the Oysters are filled with beef and horseradish jelly."

"Thank you," Lilly replied, and Charlie gave a small bow and disappeared, only to be replaced by another waiter bearing two glasses and a small bottle of champagne. Once he'd poured them each a glass, returned the bottle to the ice bucket, the neck wrapped in a monogrammed napkin, he gave a small bow and returned to the kitchen. The efficiency was breathtaking. Before tucking in, Lilly made her excuses and left in search of the bathroom.

Chapter Four

SHE SLID OPEN their carriage door and entered the corridor connection, before opening the door into the next carriage. Making her way through a couple more main carriages, she eventually reached the one she needed. This had a hall carpeted in a deep green with The Lakes Express logo woven through it in gold. There were various compartments running down the left-hand side. The first being the WC. She turned the handle and opened the door, then jumped back in shock as she found it already occupied by none other than Bobby Smith and Katherine Harp, lips locked and making out like a pair of teenagers.

"Sorry," she muttered, blushing to the roots of her hair. She closed the door and stood by the window, watching the scenery speed by while waiting for them to exit. It didn't take long.

Bobby appeared first, looking dishevelled and slightly embarrassed, while tucking in his shirt. "Sorry about that. Thought the door was locked."

Lilly nodded, but said nothing.

Then Katherine appeared, tucking a wisp of shiny red hair behind her ear. She was grinning like a Cheshire cat and obviously not embarrassed in the slightest. If anything, she seemed amused they'd been caught. She gave Lilly a wink and, without saying a word to either of them, sashayed back to her carriage, humming a jaunty tune.

Lilly locked eyes with Bobby. "You have lipstick on your neck."

His hand shot to his neck and came away crimson. "Right. Thanks," he said, taking a handkerchief from his pocket and furiously wiping away the lipstick. "Er... sorry again," he muttered, and strode away.

Lilly shook her head and entered the WC, making sure she locked the door after her. Several moments later, she was washing her hands when she overheard a raised voice coming from the brass vent in the wall behind her.

"That's your last mistake, Charlie. You're sacked."

Lilly grimaced. She rinsed her hands and took the monogrammed towel, drying her hands while she listened.

"What? You're sacking me because of an accident? Spills happen all the time. It's a moving train. I didn't do it on purpose."

"You spilled hot tea on a guest and didn't report it," the other man's voice boomed. "And it's not the first time, is it, Charlie? Finish your shift, but when we get back to Plumpton Mallet, that's the end of the line for you."

"Please give me another chance, Mr Warren. That Vincent guy doesn't like for me for some reason. I offered to pay for his dry cleaning, but he wasn't having any of it. Look, I really need this job. I promise it won't happen again."

"It's too late, lad. I'm sorry, but that's the way it is."

She heard the adjacent door open and left the WC in time to see a portly man in full uniform striding away down the corridor. She walked to the open door and, peering inside, found Charlie sitting at a small table with his head on his hands.

"Charlie?"

The young man bolted up. "I'm sorry, Madam, I didn't hear you. Can I help?"

"It's, Lilly. There's no need to be so formal. Are you all right?"

Charlie sighed. "Did you hear that?"

Lilly nodded. "I was next door, so it was hard not to."

"I've just lost my job," he said morosely. "All because that Vincent guy went ballistic when I accidentally spilled a few drops of tea on his trousers. It's not like I did it on purpose. And the tea wasn't even all that hot. It was the end of the pot. I can't believe I've got the sack over it. It's not fair."

"Are you talking about Vincent Wales? His seat is next to mine. Archie and I met him on the outward journey."

"Yeah, that's him. He's a real son of a... Sorry. Never mind. It's happened and I can't do anything about it now. Back to square one, I suppose. Look, thanks for concern, but I need to get back. They will be starting to serve dinner soon."

Lilly nodded, and said how sorry she was about what had happened, then returned to her seat.

Archie took one look at her and reached across the table to grab her hand.

"Are you all right? What's happened?"

She relayed what had happened to their waiter, Charlie and Archie frowned.

"That seems a bit harsh."

"I think so too, although according to his boss, it's not the first accident Charlie has had. But apparently Vincent made a big song and dance about it and was livid. You know, having met Vincent this morning, I find it hard to believe he'd lose his temper so badly over a little spilled tea. He seemed so personable. What do you think, Archie?"

"Actually, it doesn't surprise me at all. Remember how rude and sarcastic he was to that Katherine Harp woman?"

"Yes, I suppose so. But I'm still not wholly convinced. I realise I don't know him, but I'm usually a reasonable judge of people and it just seems a little out of character to me."

THE DINNER WAS a set meal and the first course was a pan fried turbot steak with thinly sliced potatoes, truffles and a champagne sauce. Lilly looked at Archie, shaking her head in amazement. It was arranged beautifully and tasted incredible. Alongside they were served an accompanying wine in glasses etched with The Lakes Express logo.

It was as they were eating the next course; roast fillet of lamb coated with argan oil and sweet garlic served with an oriental spice jus, and served with zucchini, aubergine, sweet peppers and tomatoes flavoured with lemon thyme, and tabbouleh and fresh peppermint leaves, that Lilly happened to glance up and see Deborah Kimble sauntering through the carriage from the far end. Lilly was about to wave and say hello when she was beaten to it by Katherine Harp, once again seated behind Archie.

"Oh, Deborah," she trilled, and Lilly saw a hand rise above Archie's head and give a little wave. Deborah joined her a moment later.

It seemed as though everyone knew Katherine Harp. *Some better than others*, she thought, remembering the scene in the bathroom.

With the background noise of animated conversations, the clinking of cutlery and the sound of the train wheels rushing along the track it shouldn't have been easy to hear the conversation, but the two women had automatically raised their voices to compensate and Lilly and Archie were privy to their exchange whether they wanted to be or not.

"How was the writer's conference, Katherine? Did you present your new novel?"

"But of course. As usual, I had a number of interested agents approach me, but I'm sticking to the one I've got. I attended the event for the PR more than anything else."

"I do love your books. They're always so exciting," Deborah gushed.

"Just you wait for the next one. It's my best yet. Even if I do say so myself."

"So, did Vincent get any offers?"

"Do you know, I have absolutely no idea," Katherine said. "I haven't seen him since we boarded the train. But he'll be around somewhere. I'll ask him when I see him."

"When is your next book out? I can hardly wait to get my hands on it."

"A few more months yet, I'm afraid. It's in the hands of my editor and he will not be rushed," Katherine sighed dramatically.

"That's a shame. I was hoping to have a new book to take on holiday with me. I don't suppose you have any recommendations, do you? Just until your new novel comes out."

Katherine laughed. "Well, personally I am a huge fan of Agatha Christie's mysteries, particularly Murder on the Orient Express. It's a real page turner and will have you guessing until the very end. It's fabulous writing. And, as you know, that's really saying something coming from me."

Lilly bit her bottom lip to prevent herself from laughing as Archie made a face at her. They both knew from the conversation that morning Katherine hadn't even read the book.

"You would have thought," Archie whispered, leaning across the table. "That she would have recommended something she'd actually read. What if she'd been quizzed on the details?"

"She'd have come up with something. She obviously thinks well on her feet. I don't know why, but I get the feeling she's trying to impress Deborah for some reason."

"Showing off more like," Archie said.

"Oh, what a wonderful idea, Katherine," they heard Deborah say. "I haven't read that book since I was in my teens. You understand my taste so well."

"I'm a writer, Deborah. It's something that comes naturally to me," Katherine replied airily.

Archie spluttered and Lilly stifled a giggle. A few moments later Deborah left to return to her husband and shortly after, Katherine rose and headed in the direction of the bar.

Lilly caught Archie's eye, and they both erupted into laughter.

"Good grief!" Archie said, as their waiter, Charlie, removed their plates and replaced them with a dessert of warm chocolate soufflé accompanied by pistachio ice-cream. "I've never heard such codswallop in my life. That woman strikes me as being nothing but a fake."

"Her books do well."

"We only have her word for that, Lilly."

"Deborah is obviously a fan."

"Probably her only one."

"Actually, I looked her up on-line after we talked to her this morning. She's very well known in the romance genre. Made a small fortune, actually."

"Really? I think I must be in the wrong line of work in that case. I still can't understand why she'd lie about reading a book when she hasn't?"

"Perhaps she's not as confident as she makes out. Vincent made more than a few cutting remarks about her writing this morning. He was very dismissive of her. That must have hurt."

"Yes, you're right. Anyway, I don't want to waste any more time talking about someone we don't know. Let's enjoy the remainder of our meal. We have a selection of cheeses next, followed by coffee and chocolate truffles."

Lilly nodded and took a mouthful of her soufflé, all thoughts of Katherine Harp vanishing from her mind as the exquisite dessert melted on her tongue.

Chapter Five

THE CHEESE COURSE was over and both of them were stuffed with Brie, Camembert, mature cheddar and Lilly's favourite Roquefort. They were just sharing the last of the truffles with a 'cheeky little Bordeaux' as Archie jokingly called it, when the train suddenly lurched. Screaming wheels and gushes of steam rose all around the train, and Lilly could hear passengers gasping and shouting in surprise as tea, wine and food were spilled. With a final screech, the train came to an abrupt halt. For a split second, there was total silence, then the complaining and raised voices began. She looked out of the window, over the soft, romantic glow of the table lamp. It was pitch black with not even a small light from a cottage, a farmhouse or a street light to be seen anywhere. They were obviously in the middle of nowhere, and judging by the time on her watch, still hours away from Plumpton Mallet.

"I don't remember a stop being on the itinerary," Archie said with a frown.

"That was definitely not planned," Lilly said. "I think the emergency handle has been pulled, Archie. I wonder why? It's a criminal offence, isn't it, unless it's for a genuine emergency?"

"Yes, I believe it is."

"What the blazes is going on?" Katherine demanded, having had more than her fair share of complimentary drinks.

"I'm sure someone will let us know shortly, dear," an elderly woman from across the aisle said, frowning at her choice of expression. But Katherine either wasn't listening or chose to ignore her.

She stood up, wobbling slightly, and looked up and down the carriage for someone in authority, but there was no one in sight. She dropped back in her seat with a huff.

A moment later, one of the train guards entered and clinked a glass with a spoon.

"Ladies and gentleman, if I could have your attention for a moment. We apologise for any inconvenience, but we are experiencing a slight technical difficulty. We expect it to be sorted out shortly and for us to be on our way. In the meantime, your servers will be around with some complimentary champagne. On behalf of The Lakes Express, we thank you all for your patience."

He hurriedly departed. To Lilly's mind, before anyone could ask pertinent questions.

She and Archie were perfectly content to talk over the champagne and another pot of coffee, but nearly an hour after the announcement, she could see some of the other passengers were becoming restless. None more so than Katherine Harp.

"Oh, come on!" she shouted. "What's going on? You can't keep us all in the dark like this. We have a right to know what's going on. We've paid good money for this trip."

Lilly heard several murmurs of agreement and was becoming concerned. She leaned over to Archie.

"I think we need to find out what's happening or we could end up with a riot on our hands. People are getting agitated and before long it could turn to anger."

"I agree. What do you suggest?"

Lilly didn't have a chance to answer as Charlie appeared with more champagne. Lilly and Archie both declined, but then Charlie leaned closer, his voice dropping to no more than a whisper.

"I'm very sorry to bother you, but I've just realised who you are, Miss Tweed. I'm from Plumpton Mallet and have read about you in the paper. You've solved a number of murder cases, haven't you?"

Lilly nodded, her stomach sinking. "Yes. Why, Charlie? Has something happened?"

He nodded. "I think you might be able to help. Would you mind?"

"No, of course not, but Archie needs to come too."

"Of course. If you'd like to follow me."

Lilly and Archie exchanged wary glances, then rose and followed Charlie through the far end of their carriage, then on through the others to the rear compartment.

"Wait here a moment, please. I need to get my boss."

Lilly recognised the man who appeared as the one who had given Charlie his marching orders earlier.

"Charlie says you're some sort of detective?" he said, speaking to Lilly.

She nodded. "I've had some experience, yes. Why what's happened?"

"One of the staff found a body and pulled the emergency brake. I tell you, in all my years aboard the TLE, I've never seen anything like it."

"I'm assuming it isn't natural causes from your reaction Mr...?"

"Warren. Kenneth Warren. And no it isn't."

"Have the police been called, Mr Warren?" Archie asked.

"Yes. But we're in the middle of nowhere, no road access unfortunately, and it will take some considerable time before they get to us, apparently."

"Wouldn't it have been better to continue onto Plumpton Mallet and let the police take over from there?" Lilly asked.

"Of course. But we're having technical difficulties. Didn't you hear the announcement?"

"Yes, but we assumed it was a ruse to hide the real reason for the stoppage. Wasn't it?" Archie said.

Mr Warren took off his cap and rubbed a hand through his sparse straw-like hair. "Sort of. There are technical difficulties once the emergency brake has been pulled. All the brakes along every carriage need to be reset again, but the train traffic controllers have to be notified, which I've already done, and then they have to come out to investigate why the brakes were activated in the first place. Legally, it's not allowed. Seeing as though we've already stopped and the reason why, both they and the police told us to stay put until they could get here."

"I see."

"Mr Warren," Lilly interrupted. "Perhaps you could show us where the body is?"

"Yes. Yes, of course. But be prepared. It's a ghastly sight."

THEY FOLLOWED KENNETH Warren to the end of the carriage, where he took out a keyring and unlocked the rear door.

"This is the former luggage compartment, but it's used for the catering supplies now."

"Was the door locked when the body was found?" Lilly asked.

"No, there's staff going in and out all the time for the food and the wine. I only locked it once I realised what had happened."

He paused, took a deep, shaky breath, and wrenched open the door.

Lilly gasped at the inert, damaged form on the floor of the carriage.

"It's Vincent Wales," she said, glancing back at Charlie, who was hovering in the doorway. He looked pale.

Archie ventured further in and, being careful not to touch anything, crouched down.

"Yes, that's Vincent all right. He's been stabbed. Repeatedly. One, two... I count twelve that I can see."

"What's that under his hand, Archie?" Lilly asked.

Archie grabbed a rubber glove from a nearby counter and, after putting it on, carefully lifted Vincent's hand to reveal a blood splattered book.

"It's the book he had with him earlier. Murder on the Orient Express. Well, it certainly looks as though he was stabbed to death."

"I don't know about that, Archie," Lilly said, coming to crouch next to him. "Look at Vincent's neck. There's definite bruising. I think he's been manually strangled." Her eye fell to the book in his hand. "Twelve stab wounds, you said?"

"You can count them if you want, but I only see twelve."

"Doesn't this all seem familiar to you, Archie?"

"Good heavens. Edward Ratchett!"

"Edward Ratchett?" Kenneth Warren said from the doorway. "Is he a passenger?"

"A book character," Lilly said. "From this book, actually. Ratchett was the victim, found dead in a sleeper car from twelve stab wounds to his chest."

"And someone thought it would be clever to put the book in his hand after they had killed him?" Mr Warren said in amazement.

Lilly shook her head. "I don't know about that. This is Vincent's book. He already had it with him. But someone is obviously trying to make a statement here. Twelve stab wounds to the chest, the train stopped in the middle of nowhere, waiting for the authorities to arrive. It's more likely they chose this method because he happened to be carrying this book. But either way, there's no doubt in my mind. We're in the middle of a deadly reenactment."

"IF WHOEVER IS responsible is trying to reenact the book, there could be some other familiar clues in here," Archie said. "Can you remember what else was part of the book, Lilly?

"A glass. In the book, Ratchett was drugged. Mr Warren, did you find a glass?"

"No. Mind you, I didn't stay long enough to look if I'm honest."

"What else, Lilly?"

"I remember matches and a handkerchief. A letter, I think. It's been a long time since I've read it. Oh, a pipe cleaner definitely. And there was something in his pocket. Archie, you've got the gloves. Would you mind going through Vincent's pockets?"

Carefully, Archie searched but came up blank. "No, there's nothing. Which in itself is a bit odd, don't you think? I've got my wallet, my glasses and some loose change in mine."

"Let's see if there's anything else to be found in here," Lilly said.

By this time, Charlie had gone back to serving the other passengers and keeping the peace, with strict instructions from Mr Warren not to breathe a word of what had happened.

Therefore, it was just the three of them who began a painstaking search of the carriage in the hopes of finding something that could point them in the direction of the murderer.

It was slow and methodical, and it wasn't until they'd almost covered the whole area that anything of import was found under one of the serving carts.

"Look at this," Lilly said, getting up from the ground where she'd been kneeling and dusting off her knees. It was a single sheet of paper, typewritten and obviously part of a larger manuscript. "*Vincent stood in the middle of the apartment and using all his detective skills took in the spectacle, committing the scene to memory...* It looks as though he named his detective after himself," Lilly said, folding the paper and putting it in her bag. "I'll keep hold of this for now and have a look at it later, but it begs the question; what happened to the rest of the manuscript? I was under the impression it was in his briefcase when he was with us this morning. Do either of you see it anywhere?"

Another look round and it was apparent the briefcase wasn't there. But they did find something else. Shoved under an old table right at the back of the room was a glass and a book of matches. Archie retrieved them with a napkin and placed them on the tabletop. "It looks as though the perpetrator is sticking to the book plot closer than we thought."

"Wait a minute. Is this where Vincent was to be served his meal, Mr Warren?" Lilly asked.

"Yes. I thought it was an extremely odd request, but he seemed a bit anxious when we boarded in the lakes and asked for somewhere quiet and private to work on the return journey. He was very insistent. This was the only space we had, but he said it was fine. It's our policy to cater to whatever a customer wants."

"Did he actually have any dinner?" Archie asked.

Mr Warren shook his head. "A staff member came to take his drinks order after everyone else had been served, and found him like this. That's when he pulled the emergency cord."

Lilly stared at the table, deep in thought. It was more than obvious that Vincent was hiding. He was certainly acting strange when he boarded, but to hide himself away in the back of the train where there were no witnesses and no one to help if he got into trouble was probably the worst decision he could have made. She turned and looked back at the body sadly.

"I know that look, Lilly," Archie said. "What are you thinking?"

"I'm just trying to process what little we know so far. The murder weapon is missing. That's the main thing. The Murder on the Orient Express book, his manuscript, the glass and matches are the only pieces of evidence we have, but apart from the manuscript, what do they actually mean? They aren't real clues like in Christie's book, are they? They've just been used to set the scene. They are no more than useless props. It's obvious someone has stolen Vincent's own book, but that's an odd motive for murder, don't you think? And why stop at just two or three of the clues used in Christie's book? It's all very strange. I can't work it out."

"Do you think the manuscript page you found could be a bit of misdirection? Whoever arranged all this has put some serious thought into it. Perhaps the briefcase didn't fit their concept?"

"No, I think the missing manuscript means something, Archie," Lilly replied. "I'm not sure it was the motive, but they took it for a reason only they know at present. It's the only real clue we have. Everything else was taken from Christie's novel, but the manuscript has nothing to do with that book. I think the page I found was most likely left in error. The killer has made their first mistake."

Chapter Six

THE THREE OF them left the carriage, and Kenneth Warren locked the door, pocketing the key.

"Are you the only one with a key?" Lilly asked.

"My second has one, but he's aware of the situation and has no intention of using it. What do you want to do now?"

"I'd like your second's key, please. We will no doubt have to visit the crime scene again."

"Yes, I can let you have that. Anything else you want me to do?"

"I think the first thing is for you to inform the other passengers that a serious crime has been committed and we won't be going anywhere until the authorities arrive, Mr Warren." Lilly said. "I can't speak as to the others, but those in our carriage were beginning to get annoyed at the delay when we left to come here. It could be a lot worse now."

"I'd also stop the alcohol you're serving," Archie said. "I'd suggest tea, coffee and water from now on or we'll end up with a few fights on our hands."

"I've already given orders to that effect."

"Do you have enough supplies without reentering the crime scene?"

"We do. It's all in the kitchens. Although, if we are here for an extended period we may need more food."

"All right," Lilly said. "We'll cross that bridge when we come to it. I think Archie and I need to start speaking to a few people. Do you have somewhere private where we can conduct interviews?"

"You can use the first-class staff lounge. It's just up here."

Lilly and Archie followed him back up the train carriage to a simple, but cosy and clean compartment where there was a table and several armchairs set out alongside a bank of staff lockers. It was the room where Mr Warren had sacked Charlie and Lilly had overheard from the WC next door.

"This will do fine, Mr Warren. Thank you. Do you think you can spare Charlie to assist in escorting the passengers we want to speak to?"

Mr Warren hesitated. "Charlie?"

"Yes. He's been our personal server whilst on board this evening and he's very efficient and polite and strikes me as being both bright and discreet."

"Oh, well, yes, of course. Who do you want to start with?"

"I think, considering the altercation between the writer Katherine Harp and Vincent Wales about Agatha Christie's book this morning, we should start with her," Lilly said.

"He talked to her about the book this morning?" Mr Warren asked.

"He did," Archie confirmed. "And he was particularly offensive about the type of books she herself writes. Called them smut."

"I wouldn't call them that," Kenneth Warren said, then blushed when he realised what he'd said.

Lilly smiled. "Katherine's books are obviously more popular than I'd realised. I think we're ready now, if you could arrange for Charlie to bring her here."

"I'll do it straight away. I must also thank you both for agreeing to help. If you can manage to perhaps not solve the case, but make some decent headway before the police arrive, we might actually make it back to Plumpton Mallet before breakfast. Otherwise, we're all in for a very long night."

"Oh, there's just one other thing, Mr Warren," Lilly said. "Excuse my ignorance, but I know nothing about steam trains. Are we likely to lose the heat and the power now the train is no longer moving?"

Mr Warren smiled indulgently. "No, don't worry, it's not like the old days. We have a back-up generator and batteries that should see us through for ten hours at least. Although I hope we won't be stuck here for that long or we'll all be on rations."

***

"I'M BEGINNING TO feel a bit like Hercule Poirot myself," Lilly said as they sat waiting for Katherine to arrive.

"No, your moustaches aren't nearly so magnificent."

Lilly burst out laughing. "Archie Brown! Are you saying I've got a moustache?"

"Of course not. Can I have a look at that bit of manuscript you found while we're waiting?"

Lilly retrieved it from her handbag and passed it over.

"Reads a bit like the old pulp crime fiction from the 50s. You can't glean much about the book from one page, it's just describing the ubiquitous femme fatale... oh, my word!"

"What?"

Archie passed the page back. "Look at the last paragraph."

He didn't cross paths with a woman of this calibre often, one with curves in all the right places, and he knew she was going to be trouble in more ways than one. "Katie," she purred, holding out her hand. So this was the romance dame he'd heard so much about. Katie Hart, known for her sharp wit as well as her

The rest of the sentence was missing, obviously on the next page, but Lilly had read enough to know who he meant.

"Well, that's not a coincidence, is it?"

"Hardly. And depending on how he's portrayed her in the rest of the book, it could very well be a motive."

"I don't want to jump to any conclusions just yet, Archie, but it does make her a person of interest, as they say in the movies."

There was a sharp rap on the door, and Charlie opened it. "I've brought Ms Harp to see you."

"Thank you, Charlie."

Katherine walked in while Archie said goodbye to Charlie and closed the door.

"So what's this all about?" she asked, swinging her red hair over one shoulder.

"Have a seat, Katherine," Archie said, sitting himself and taking a notebook and pen from his inside jacket pocket. "We've just got a few questions. But first, can you walk us through your evening since you arrived back on the train?"

She folded her arms and shook her head. "No, I don't think so. Not until I know what this is all about."

"We really would appreciate your help, Katherine," Lilly said, trying to appeal to her woman to woman. She should have known it wasn't going to work.

"And I would appreciate knowing why two amateur sleuths suddenly think they have the authority to be interrogating people." She decided then to sit, and pointed an accusing finger at Lilly as she did so. "I realised later who you were. I've seen the articles in the paper that your friend here wrote. Now, I know it's something serious because we've just been told we have to wait for the police to arrive before we can move again, but I'm not answering any of your questions until you answer one of mine. What has happened to make the train stop?"

She's good, Lilly thought, amused.

"All right. Earlier this evening, Vincent Wales was found dead. He's been murdered."

Katherine's eyes widened and she slumped against the back of the chair, hand on her heart. "What?"

"Vincent has been killed, Katherine. We're talking to everyone to see if we can find out who did it."

"And you're starting with me? Why?"

Archie leaned back in his chair, choosing to let Lilly take the lead.

Lilly put the sheet of paper on the table between them.

"Did you ever read Vincent's recent manuscript?"

"No," she said, picking the page up.

"Read the last paragraph. I think you'll find it interesting."

Katherine sighed impatiently but began to read. Her expression changed when she spotted the name of the female character.

"He made me a character. How amusing. But he never liked me, you know? I bet the woman dies a horrible death. It's a murder mystery, after all. Where's the rest of the book? I wouldn't mind reading it to see if I'm right."

"The manuscript is missing. This was left behind. By accident or design, we don't know yet," Archie said.

"You think whoever killed him stole his manuscript?"

"It's possible the theft of the manuscript was the motive," Lilly said.

Katherine finally began to look nervous.

"So, you're saying just because he based a character on me, I decided to steal the manuscript and kill him? Is that what you're saying? Because I haven't even read the manuscript until this bit and I didn't know he'd put me in it. And why would I even want it? It's a crime novel. I write romance in case you've forgotten. You're grasping at straws."

"You could have stolen it to prevent it from being

published," Archie said. "Assuming there's information in there you don't want to get out."

"You obviously have some sort of past relationship, Katherine," Lilly added. "If the tense conversation on the train this morning is anything to go by."

To Lilly's surprise, Katherine laughed with what appeared to be genuine amusement.

"You mean the part where Vincent accused me of being stupid without actually saying it? I'm hardly going to take anything he says seriously. Just because he's writing a murder mystery, and not a very good one if this is any indication," she said, pointing to the page on the table, "he thinks he's going to be the next break out novelist. He just thinks he's better than me because of my genre. But guess what? I'm the one with the huge following and my sales are doing very nicely, thank you. I have absolutely no complaints."

"He seemed to get under your skin," Lilly said, refusing to let it drop.

"He most certainly did not."

"We over heard you speaking to Deborah Kimble about Murder on the Orient Express. You told her you'd read it before, yet earlier you said you hadn't."

"I read it over lunch at the conference."

Lilly just stared at her. It was obvious Katherine was lying. Not only would the conference have kept her too busy to read, but she couldn't imagine her being able to get through a book of over two hundred and fifty pages during a one hour lunch break. Even if she had sat alone and spoke to no one the entire time.

"So what part of the book was your favourite?"

Katherine crossed her arms and glared at Lilly.

"Are you testing me?"

"Yes," Lilly said bluntly. "I don't believe you read the book at all. It would be impossible in the time you had. And if you are lying about that, it makes me question what else you're lying about?"

Katherine threw both hands up in the air.

"Okay, fine! I read the cliff notes, so sue me! I let Vincent get under my skin about the book. Is that what you want to hear? It was stupid. I decided to see what the fuss was all about, but I was busy, so I just picked up details about the plot and characters on-line. When Deborah asked for a recommendation, it was the first thing that popped into my head. It means nothing."

"I realise it's probably difficult," Archie said, resting his arms on the table and leaning towards Katherine. "But you shouldn't have let him bother you so much. He was rude and offensive to you this morning. It was uncalled for. But I get the sense there's more to the story than you're saying. What exactly happened between the two of you?"

"Oh, for heaven's sake. Not that it's any of your business, but we were an item for a while. It was ages ago. It was a brief affair. I'm not one for long-term relationships, and Vincent was emotionally needy on the one hand and supercilious on the other. It drove me mad. It's going to take someone far more impressive and much less mercurial to win me over."

"Katherine," Lilly said. "I get the impression you know a lot more than you're letting on."

The woman shrugged in response. "You can think what you like. I know nothing of what's happened on this train, or why. And if you seriously think a fictitious character based on me means anything other than my ex is still harbouring bitter feelings about the split and probably decided to kill me off in his book, then you're deluded."

"We don't know enough about Vincent's book to assume your character is the victim. Unless you've read it before."

Katherine scoffed loudly. "I think this mockery of an interrogation is over. I don't like being accused of something I didn't do. We're finished here." She stood up, flinging back her hair and stormed out of the carriage, slamming the door in her wake. But not before Archie told her to keep quiet about everything.

"WELL, DIDN'T THAT go well?" Archie said. "I hope everyone we speak to is as nice and accommodating as that."

Lilly couldn't help but laugh at his sarcasm. "It was interesting though," he continued. "Although, I'm surprised at how grubby I'm feeling prying into someone else's private life like this. You'd think it was par for the course in my line of work, wouldn't you?"

"We've only just started, I'm afraid, Archie."

"Don't I know it," he muttered.

"So, what did you think?"

"You gave her quite a bit of information. Are you sure that was wise? I hope she keeps her mouth shut like we asked her to."

"We didn't tell her anything about how Vincent was found or how he was killed. I'm keeping those details secret for now. But we did learn something significant."

"The fact she and him were an item," Archie said, nodding. "She wasn't very nice about him though, was she?"

"We've only got her word for it that Vincent was prone to mood swings. It's not as though he's able to defend himself."

"No. And we're assuming by the way she spoke that it was she who instigated the breakup. It might have been him, you know."

"Yes, it might have been. Katherine Harp is definitely on my 'possible' list. She was wandering around all over chatting with people, so certainly had the opportunity. But then again, she did seem genuinely surprised that she'd been used as a character in Vincent's novel. It makes me think if it was her who killed him, then the manuscript wasn't the motive. But, another thing that struck me was that never once did she refer to Vincent in the past tense. I know it seems like a cliché, something you would read in a book, but I noticed it almost straightaway."

"Mmm," said Archie. "I suppose you could attach some significance to it. Or it could just mean she's just clever. Cleverer than Vincent thought she was, anyway. How do we find out if she, or anybody else for that matter, has an alibi? I mean, without knowing there'd been a murder in the first place, it's difficult to work it out. I wasn't taking much notice of anyone in particular, were you?" Lilly shook her head. "People were up and down to the bathroom, the bar, stretching their legs, chatting at other tables and in other carriages. How are we supposed to sort through it all, Lilly?"

"One forward step at a time, Archie. It's all we can do. Talk to people, ask as many questions as we can and see if something falls into place. We need to at least try to work out the time he was killed. Or as close as we can, anyway. That will give us a place to start. We know it was around dinner time, and that he was to be served after every once else. So I suppose we're as close as we can be. Now we need to find out where certain people were at that time."

"All right. So who's next?"

"I think Bobby Smith. Vincent was definitely nervous when the man turned up in our carriage and made a hasty exit as soon as he did. He came back from the hotel and hid in the catering carriage immediately. And I also caught Bobby and Katherine in the bathroom together just as the canapés were served. I'll leave you to imagine what they were doing."

"Good grief, really?"

"Yes, really."

"Why didn't you tell me?"

"It slipped my mind. I'd just heard Charlie getting sacked and forgot all about those two."

"Incidentally, why did you ask for Charlie specifically to help us?"

Lilly shrugged. "I feel sorry for him. According to what I overheard, he really needs this job. He was distraught when I found him afterwards. I suppose I thought I was helping him in front of Kenneth Warren. If he knows how good Charlie is at his job, he might reconsider."

"You're too soft hearted sometimes, Lilly. But I admire your sense of justice. So, what are your thoughts about Bobby Smith?"

"I'm wondering if Bobby is the reason Vincent was hiding. It certainly seemed like it. Perhaps there's some sort of rivalry between the ex and the man who is Katherine's current fling?"

"Well, let's bring him in and ask. But first I need a drink. I'll go and find Charlie and ask him to arrange a pot of coffee for us before he goes and gets Mr Smith. Is that all right with you?"

"That's fine with me, Archie. I'm parched with all this talking, and I need the jolt of caffeine to keep me awake."

Archie had only just reached the door when there was a brief knock and Charlie entered.

"I saw Miss Harp return and came to see who you needed next? Was it her then, do you think?"

"It's far too early to say, Charlie," Lilly said with a smile. "Could you bring Bobby Smith next? I don't know where his seat is, but you might find him in the bar."

"I'll check the passenger manifest. No problem, I'll find him. Anything else?"

"Did Miss Harp go straight back to her seat, do you know? She's not talking to anyone else, is she?" Lilly said, hoping she and Bobby Smith hadn't crossed paths and were at that very moment getting their stories straight between them.

"No, she's on her own at her table, reading a book. That it?"

"Could we have a large pot of coffee, if you don't mind?" Archie added.

"Coming right up," Charlie said, and disappeared.

"He makes a very good assistant, doesn't he?" Archie said with a smile

THE COFFEE, ALONG with a covered silver salver containing a selection of sandwiches, was brought in on a wheeled cart by a smart waiter, who gave a small bow and retreated in silence.

"You can't fault the service," Archie said, pouring the coffee and handing a cup to Lilly. "Although after what we've eaten today, I don't think I can manage a sandwich just yet."

"I can't either at the moment. But they'll keep. How do you want to play this interview, Archie? Bobby struck me as a bit of a man's man, plus I caught him in a compromising position so he might not want to speak to me. Do you want to lead?"

"Fine by me. And if we find he does actually respond better to you, then you can take over."

Bobby Smith was in a dishevelled state when he arrived and took a seat before them, stretching out his legs and folding his hands over a slight paunch, but there was an amused glint in his eye as though he wasn't taking anything seriously. *So much for him being embarrassed*, Lilly thought.

"Well, you two aren't the fuzz, are you?" He said and roared with laughter. "What is this, amateur hour?"

Lilly smiled thinly. "Something like that."

"Mr Smith," Archie said. "We've been asked to help in an official capacity, by the manager of the train, regarding an incident which took place this evening."

"What incident? Someone stealing the booze?"

"I understand you know Vincent Wales?" Archie said, ignoring the man's question.

"That idiot? What's he done, fallen off the train? Is that why we've stopped?" he said with a sneer.

"Earlier this evening, Vincent Wales was found dead, Mr Smith."

"Dead?" he said, looking from Lilly to Archie and back again. "You're having a laugh, aren't you?"

When neither of them spoke, just stared at him in silence, Bobby Smith's demeanor changed as the seriousness of the situation slowly sank into his whiskey fogged brain. The smile faded, and he sat up straight.

"How did it happen? A heart-attack was it?"

Archie shook his head. "I'm sorry to say that Mr Wales was murdered."

"Murdered?" he said, with a stunned look on his face. "How?"

"I can't give you any details at the moment," Archie said. "But I understand you knew him?"

Bobby nodded. "Yeah, I did. Through Katherine. Murdered! Hell's bells, I can't believe it."

"Why was Vincent so uncomfortable the moment he saw you this morning?" Lilly asked.

Bobby sighed. "We've got a bit of history, him and me. Honestly? The guy was a total arse. I know you shouldn't speak ill of the dead and all that, but I don't believe in that rubbish. He was a complete git when he was alive and that's all that matters, right? I'm not saying I'm glad he's dead, I'm not. I wouldn't wish that on my worst enemy, but I don't get the point of making someone out to be nice when they weren't, just because they've happened to pop their clogs."

"Can you start at the beginning, Bobby?" Archie said. "How well did you know him?"

Bobby shrugged. "Not all that well to start with. We lived in the same town as it happens and frequented the same watering hole, so I knew him to nod to, but we didn't talk much. He wasn't my sort of bloke, to be honest. Too artsy fartsy and full of himself. You could tell he thought he was better than everyone else. Anyway, there was one night when he was there and Katherine was with him. He introduced us and we started chatting. She was good company, fun to be around, you know? I couldn't understand what she saw in Vincent, but it wasn't any of my business. A couple of weeks later, Friday night, I'm back in there playing darts with some of the lads and in she walks. Well, I could tell straight off she was upset, so went over and offered to buy her drink."

"Was it something to do with Vincent?"

"Yeah. He'd broken up with her." Lilly glanced quickly at Archie, who nodded briefly. "But she didn't live there, see? She was from around Lincoln somewhere and had travelled up to see him and stay the weekend. Now he'd kicked her out, and she had nowhere to go. So, me being the gentleman I was, I offered her my sofa."

"Right. Naturally." Archie said and cleared his throat. "So why did Vincent call it off?"

"Because he said she was thick. An ignorant moron who had nothing but fresh air between her ears and was embarrassing to be seen with in public once she'd opened her mouth. You can see now why I think he's a pig. You have no idea what that did to her confidence. She was a mess. It took me nearly all night to convince her it wasn't true, but I did it. We've been friends ever since."

"I believe you are more than friends," Lilly said. "Wouldn't you say?"

To his credit, Bobby blushed again. "Well yes, all right. Let's call it 'friends with benefits,' shall we? We're not officially dating or anything like that."

"It still doesn't explain why Vincent made himself scarce when you appeared, though," Archie said.

"Yeah, I was getting to that. So, fast forward a few weeks and I'm back in the pub, and who should strut in, but Mr high and mighty himself, Vincent Wales. I hadn't clapped eyes on the bloke since the night he'd ditched Katherine and my blood started to boil. I just stood and stared at him. Eventually he asks what my problem is and I tell him how badly I thought he'd treated Katherine. Not in those words you understand. I wasn't that polite about it. But you get the drift. Anyway, I couldn't believe it, but he started to laugh."

"That scoundrel!" Archie blurted out, unable to help himself and causing Bobby and Lilly to jump.

"Er, right," Bobby said, eyeing Archie with undisguised curiosity.

Lilly smiled to herself. It was an archaic word, and she doubted Bobby had ever heard anyone use it before. But that was Archie, she thought warmly. A real, almost old-fashioned gentleman.

"Anyway," Bobby continued. "I called him a lot worse. Told him he ought to be ashamed of himself for treating a lady so badly. And do you know what he said? He said, *she's about as far from a lady as you can get. She's nothing but a two bit smut writer who can barely string a sentence together.* Well, I wasn't having that. I punched his lights out. He hit the floor like a sack of spuds, wailing like a kid. I half expected him to cry out for his mummy."

"That would certainly explain why he dashed off when he saw you this morning. Especially considering he'd all but accused Katherine of being stupid, again," Lilly said and Bobby nodded.

"Did you and Vincent speak at all today?" Archie asked.

"Nah, but I saw him. I'd got a ticket to the writer's thing because Katherine was on a panel and I wanted to see her in action as it were, but I ended up in another room where a bunch of writers were making pitches to publishers and agents. I found it interesting, so stuck around for a while."

"And that's where you saw Vincent?"

"That's right. He was in a corner talking to two or three publishing company reps about his book. They looked pretty interested, so I wandered over. I was curious. As it happened, they were wrapping up so I didn't learn much. Two of the reps gave Vincent their cards, saying they were very interested. He looked pleased with himself. Then he saw me." Bobby laughed. "He looked nervous and quickly packed up and left."

"But you didn't speak?" Archie asked.

"Nope. I just glared at him and he ran away. So I left and went to find Katherine."

"Bobby," Lilly said. "Can you remember anything at all about what was discussed? Anything about the book itself or the characters, for instance? Maybe the title?"

Bobby looked up, obviously thinking back.

"Actually, Vincent had brought a mock-up of the cover with him, and I remember one guy telling him their in-house art department would be responsible for that if they took the book on."

"What did it look like?" Archie asked, pen poised over his notebook.

"Not too bad actually, although the rep said it was a bit of a cliché. But what do I know? It was the silhouette of a woman sprawled out on a red sofa, arm dangling like she was dead and a magnifying glass on the floor. The title was 'Death of a Scarlet Woman.'"

Lilly nodded, thinking perhaps Katherine was right after all and Vincent had killed her off in the book.

Archie had his head down, making notes in shorthand, and without looking up asked Bobby if he'd seen or spoken to Vincent since returning to the train that evening?

"No. I heard he'd boarded but never saw him. I headed straight for the bar and stayed there until a got a text from Katherine asking her to meet me..." He looked at Lilly with a smirk, no longer embarrassed at being caught. "Well, you know what happened then."

"Did you go back to your seat afterwards?"

"Actually, I went back to the bar. No point in wasting free drinks, right? That's where I had dinner. Then the train stopped and here we are. Is that it then?"

Lilly nodded. "Yes, I think so. We'll call you if we think of anything else. Thank you."

Chapter Seven

"HE'S JUST ONE big walking, talking cliché, isn't he?" Archie said once Bobby had left.

Lilly laughed. "I swear he thought you were talking Swahili or something when you called Vincent a Scoundrel."

"What's wrong with scoundrel?"

"Absolutely nothing, Archie. Nothing at all. It makes you sound dashing."

Archie looked at her and raised an eyebrow, a slow smile creeping across his face until it became a full-blown grin.

"Are you taking the mickey, by any chance?"

"Of course not," she replied, grinning back at him. "Just don't start with cad or bounder, or I won't be able to keep a straight face."

"That's a shame. I had plans for those. And I was sure I could slip mangy cur or hornswoggler into the conversation somewhere. Oh well, never mind. I'll have to be content with keeping my linguistic prowess under the proverbial bushel for now. So, cliché aside, do we think he's a murderer?"

Lilly thought for a moment, then shrugged.

"I honestly don't know at this stage, Archie. My gut reaction says he certainly was angry enough at the way Vincent had treated Katherine to punch him, so he's not above getting physical. But whether he's capable of murder is something different all together. We'll just have to keep gathering as much information as we can and see where it goes."

"Fancy a break before we carry on? You look as though you could do with it. Are you all right?"

"I'm fine. I just can't believe I've become embroiled in yet another murder investigation."

"You have a good reputation for solving them, though, Lilly. That's why you were asked this time. And at least we're doing it together."

"Yes, I suppose so. And thanks for taking all the notes. You're much better at short-hand than I am. I'm very glad you're here, Archie. Anyway, in answer to your first question, yes, I think a bit of a break is a good idea. I need to stretch my legs."

She left the compartment where Archie had opened the salver and was tucking into smoked salmon and watercress sandwiches, and walked down to the staff bathroom. No matter what she had told Archie, Lilly was still upset that she was investigating a murder on what was supposed to be a pleasurable trip for them both. It was their first real date and now it was spoiled. Then she felt guilty knowing that poor Vincent Wales would never again have a holiday or a date with someone new. And wouldn't see the book he was so proud of published and in the hands of readers and fans.

She washed her hands, then inspected her reflection in the small art deco mirror above the sink.

"Oh, my god, what a fright!" she said aloud, rummaging around in her handbag for a hairbrush.

She hadn't given a single thought to what she looked like since they'd boarded the train that morning. Since then, she'd walked for hours and been blown about and soaked in a boat. Consequently, her hair was stuck up in several directions, and plastered down in others. She looked like Worzel Gummidge. She couldn't help but smile at the fact Archie had never once said she looked a mess. As she searched for a brush, she came across a small velvet pouch. It was her travel supply of tea. She put it on the edge of the sink. She'd go and ask for a pot of hot water when she'd finished. She could do with a cup of Oat Straw tea. She'd thought this blend would be a good one to have with her today, as it reduced fatigue. Luckily, considering what she was now doing, studies suggested it was also good for improving attention and concentration.

With her hair brushed and lipstick reapplied, she left the bathroom and went up to the kitchens. The 'working' part of the first-class section was situated in a single carriage, so there wasn't far to go. She caught a waiter with a tray and asked if he could bring a pot of hot water and some fresh cups to the staff lounge when he had a free moment?

"Certainly, Madam. Will you require anything else?"

"No, that's all for now. Thank you," she replied and returned to Archie.

"**Y**OU LOOK BETTER, Lilly."

"I couldn't have looked any worse, let's be honest. Why didn't you tell me I looked a complete shambles, Archie?"

"A shambles? You never look like that, Lilly. Whatever do you mean?"

She could see he was genuinely confused, and it made her smile. She walked over and gave him a kiss on the cheek.

"Thank you, Archie. Just ignore me. I don't mean anything."

"All right. Well, I also need to pay a visit before we continue. Back in a tick. I've left you some sandwiches, by the way. They're excellent."

By the time Archie returned, Lilly had finished the food and a pot of hot water and two cups had replaced the cart of coffee.

"What's this?" Archie asked, returning to his seat.

"Oat Straw tea. I always carry a stash of something with me. Do you want a cup?"

"Absolutely. I think I've had enough coffee for today. So, who's in the hot seat next?"

"I think it has to be Charlie."

"Ah, yes, our efficient, yet soon to be unemployed, assistant. Do you think that's motive enough? And what about how the murder has been staged?"

"We certainly can't ignore the fact he lost his job because of Vincent, and then Vincent is murdered not more than an hour later. When I spoke to him, he was very upset, begging Mr Warren to allow him to keep his job. He intimated life would be very difficult without any work. Regarding the links to the Agatha Christie book, at the moment I can't see why he would have done that, but I don't really know anything about him."

"But you feel sorry for him even though he's a suspect. I know."

Lilly took a mouthful of tea and sighed in contentment.

"There's a bit more to it than that. Two more reasons, actually. The first being what I told Mr Warren, he's an intelligent and efficient, likable young man who could help us. The second because if he is our culprit, I want to keep him close and let him lower his guard."

"You devious woman, Lilly Tweed! What on earth gave you that idea?"

Lilly grinned. "Would you believe a book?"

"Don't tell me an Agatha Christie novel?"

"Got it in one, Mr Brown. Although not the one that's central to this investigation."

Archie laughed, highly amused.

"How ironic. You know, Lilly, I really do think you're going to solve this case. If anyone can find out what happened to Vincent Wales, it's you. I'm just along for the ride. Captain Hastings to your Poirot."

"But without the moustache."

THERE WAS NO need to go in search of Charlie, as Lilly had told Archie when he offered to go and find him. He turned up of his own accord not long after he'd realised Bobby Smith had returned to the bar.

"Come on in, Charlie," she said. "Have a seat."

He paused for a moment, then nodded and came and sat in front of them.

"I wondered when you were going to get around to me. Look, before you start, I just want to say something. I might only be a waiter on a train, not a doctor or a solicitor, but I'm not stupid. I've seen enough crime shows on TV to know how this works. You'll ask me loads of questions, putting words in my mouth until I confess. Well, you'll be disappointed. No matter how many different ways you ask me the same question, my answer will be the same. No, I did not kill Vincent Wales. Yes, he was a horrible man, and he cost me my job, but do you think I'd kill him when that would only make things a thousand times worse? All right, at the end of this journey I'll not have a job, and I really need one. But killing a man over a bit of spilled tea is ridiculous, and would mean I'd never get another position. I just wouldn't do it. I couldn't do it. It makes me feel sick thinking about murdering someone."

Lilly nodded. It all sounded very plausible, and if she was being honest, she really didn't think Charlie had it in him to kill anybody. But, at the moment, he was a suspect and if she was to do her job properly, then he needed to be questioned, if for no other reason than to eliminate him.

"Charlie, let's just make things clear. This is not an interrogation. You are not under arrest. It's just an interview, a conversation, so we can get the facts and try to find out what happened. I understand completely what you've just said, and honestly, I find it very hard to believe you're the one who killed Vincent, but I need your side of the story so I can eliminate you and start to concentrate on finding who really did commit this murder. Do you understand?"

Charlie breathed a sigh of relief and leaned back in his chair, giving Lilly a smile.

"Yes, I understand. Okay, what do you want to know?"

"Have you ever read the book Murder on the Orient Express by Agatha Christie?"

Charlie nodded. "Yes, in school. I can't really remember much about it, only that I didn't like it very much. It was a bit boring. I know Vincent Wales had a copy in his hand when you found him though, and that the scene was made to look like the book."

Lilly nodded. It was pointless trying to keep details of the crime scene from him when he'd been there, so she tried a different approach.

"Tell me about the incident with the spilled tea."

Some unintended tone in her voice must have set Charlie's internal alarm ringing, because he suddenly threw up his arms and said, "All right fine, I lied. I suppose Mr Warren has told you?"

Lilly didn't know what he was talking about, but didn't admit it. This could be pertinent information.

"I'd like to hear it in your own words, Charlie."

"I don't suppose it matters now. I've already lost my job. The truth is I poured hot tea in his lap on purpose."

Lilly nodded, as though she already knew all about it.

"The question is why, Charlie?"

"I DON'T SUPPOSE I could have a cup of tea too, could I?" Charlie asked, eyeing Lilly's cup.

"Yes, of course you can, but it's one of my own blends, Oat Straw. I'm not sure if you'll like it."

"It'll be fine. I'm just thirsty and don't want to go down to the kitchen for one. Thank you." He took a tentative sip and nodded. "It's all right, actually. Different, but not bad."

"So what happened for you to pour tea on Vincent, Charlie?" Archie asked, pen poised over his notebook.

"I hadn't been in the job long when I first met him. He was taking the trip to go to another writer's conference at the same hotel you were at today. They run them regularly and he always goes. Anyway, he asked if I could spare some time to talk to him."

Charlie went on to explain how weird he thought it was that a passenger wanted to talk to a waiter. He had no idea what it was about, but as the company's motto is to keep the passengers happy, he said yes. Although he insisted it had to be during his break.

His break came and Vincent Wales was waiting for him.

"Basically, it was like an interview. He wanted to know how I got the job, what the interview was like, what my job and responsibilities were. Why I wanted to work on a train in the first place? Had I ever had difficult passengers and what I did about it? How things actually worked on the train, who my boss was. Everything really."

"Why did he want to know all that, Charlie?" Lilly asked.

"He said he was writing a book based on a train and the main character was a waiter. It was for research because he wanted to get all the details right. I didn't think anything of it to start with."

"So what happened?"

"He wrote the story and put it on his blog. I don't know if you've seen it, but it's got a lot of followers. It was re-blogged all over the place."

"What was the story about?" Archie asked.

"A waiter on a train who was a drug addict and stole from the passengers to buy the drugs. It ended with him beating a passenger half to death and going to prison."

"Did he use your actual name? Lilly said.

"He was called Chaz, no surname."

It's like pulling teeth, Lilly thought in frustration.

"So if he didn't name you, what was your problem with him? It must have been more than that?"

"Because he used my picture without my permission! He took a photo of me on the platform surrounded by steam, in my uniform helping a passenger off the train, and used it as the book cover. It was all over his stupid blog and my parents saw it. My girlfriend and my friends saw it! I nearly lost my job because people thought it was true. My dad was furious and my mum was really upset. They thought I was taking drugs and stealing! My girlfriend dumped me and I would have lost my job if I hadn't managed to persuade Mr Warren it was all lies. As it was, I had to take numerous drug tests to prove it every time I came on shift. He made my life hell and didn't care."

"I'm sorry, Charlie," Lilly said. "I assume your parents and family and friends know it was fiction now, do they?"

Charlie nodded. "Yeah, but now he's dead and I've lost my job, it's going to bring it all back. I don't think I can go through it all again. It was bad enough the first time. Damn, I wish I hadn't poured tea on him. But he made me so mad."

Lilly glanced at Archie, then back at Charlie.

"What did he do to make you angry today?"

"He made a joke about taking my picture again for another story. Even had his phone out ready. If I hadn't had my hands full with the cup and the tea pot, I'd have snatched it off him. As it was, I did the only thing I could to make him stop."

"You poured tea in his lap?"

Charlie nodded and looked down at the table. "I tried to make out it was an accident, but he knew it wasn't. He complained to Mr Warren, and I lost my job. You know the rest."

Chapter Eight

"WELL," SAID ARCHIE, after Charlie had gone. "It seems our young assistant has a bit of temper."

"I don't in any way condone what he did. That tea could have caused serious burning, and it was right that he lost his job as a result. He's lucky he isn't being charged with assault. But I do understand why he was so furious."

"Oh, don't get me wrong, so do I, Lilly. But, like you say, this was entirely the wrong action for him to take. Obviously it was done on the spur of the moment, in blind anger, but it did cross my mind that in order to avoid the more serious charge of assault, he could have killed Vincent to get him out of the way once and for all. What do you think?"

"I hate to admit it, but I think that's more than feasible. That could very well be Charlie's motive. But we really need, now more than ever, to get the time of death as near as possible, because Charlie was serving us at dinner."

"Mmm. But he was dashing back and forth to the kitchen, and waiting for us to finish our courses. He wasn't with us all the time, Lilly. He could have gone to the rear of the carriage. But whether he had time to strangle, then stab Vincent and put out the props, take the manuscript and be back in time to serve our next course, I don't know."

"Neither do I."

"So, who do we talk to next?"

"The staff to start with, then the other passengers. Someone must have seen something, Archie, even if they didn't realise it was important at the time. These carriages are for staff only. They are the working parts of the train and as such, no passenger should be here for any reason except to use the WC, which is the very first door. We need to see if anyone remembers someone entering who wasn't using the facilities or didn't belong."

Archie nodded. "Good idea. Especially as we seem to have run out of suspects to interview."

Lilly pulled a face. "Yes. That too."

They went in search of Kenneth Warren, who gave them permission to speak to whomever they needed. They started with the kitchen staff and then the servers, none of whom remembered anything out of the ordinary. But they all said the same thing: they were extremely busy preparing and serving food. Taking orders for drinks, getting the orders from the bar and taking them back to the passenger's tables. In short, they were all so busy doing their jobs that they weren't taking any notice of what was going on around them, save what the customer they were serving at the time wanted.

Lilly and Archie moved onto the carriage nearest to where Vincent was found, and began to talk to the passengers. She started with a large, florid man, with a slightly wonky ginger moustache, called Barney, who said he spent most of his time in the bar before dinner, only returning to his seat to eat when his server came to find him. Another lady, along with her husband, said they were too busy playing cards to take any notice of what was around them. After conversations with several others, all of them saying they hadn't seen or heard anything, Archie was becoming frustrated.

"Is it too much to ask that *someone* saw *something*?" he muttered behind Lilly.

Those they'd spoken to so far had left their assigned seats at one time or another to go to the bar or meet up with friends in other carriages, so were too far from the scene of the crime. But because they didn't have an exact time of death, it was difficult to ascertain who had alibis and who didn't. It wasn't until they reached the end of the carriage and an elderly lady with a shock of white hair and a permanent twinkle in her periwinkle blue eye that they got any useful information at all.

Millicent Hardacre was travelling alone and at a table for two, where the seat opposite was vacant. Lilly introduced herself and Archie and explained the reason they were there.

"Ms Hardacre," Archie began, crouching in the aisle so he could look her in the eye, while Lilly sat opposite.

"Oh, call me Milly, dear."

Archie smiled. "Milly, it would appear that you are one of the few people who remained in your seat this evening."

"That's right, young man. I'm not too steady on my feet nowadays, I'm afraid. It's my hip, you know. I'm on the waiting list for a replacement, but in the meantime, I rest when I can."

"Did you walk into the town when we arrived at the lakes?" Lilly asked, wondering how this sweet old lady would have managed on her own.

"Oh, I didn't leave the train at all, my dear. They're quite happy to let me stay on, you know. I've made this trip many times. It's one of my favourites. In the old days, I walked down there, but I've seen it all before. No, I just love the train journey itself. It reminds me of my youth," she said with a dreamy smile.

"Milly, did you happen to hear or see anything in the next carriage?" Lilly asked, although she knew what the answer would be. Milly Hardacre, as bright as she was, was obviously hard of hearing. Lilly had already noticed a hearing aid in each ear and she was simply too far away from the carriage where it had happened. But to her surprise, Milly looked around her then turned back to them both with a smile.

"Would you mind if I stretched my legs a little? I've been sitting down for quite a long time now. I need to get the blood pumping in these old legs of mine again."

She proceeded to grab the walking cane where it was hooked over the arm of her seat, and without waiting for a response, set off slowly and with a pronounced gait as she favoured her dodgy hip, back up the carriage in the direction Lilly had Archie had come from.

"*N*OW THEN, MY dears," she said, once they'd left the carriage and were standing in the hallway of the adjacent one. "I know something serious has happened or the train wouldn't have stopped like it has. Nor would you be interviewing the passengers. Is there somewhere we can go to talk privately? It's not that I know anything in particular, but I'd rather not be overheard. One never knows who is listening. Especially now the train has come to a standstill. It's very quiet, isn't it, without the wheels in motion?"

"Very wise, Milly," Archie said. "I should have thought of that myself. We have been conducting interviews in the staff lounge. It's just up here. Would you like tea while we talk?"

Milly shook her head. "No. No tea. I think a small sherry is called for, if you wouldn't mind?"

Archie caught Lilly's eye and grinned at her over Milly's head. "I'll see to it straight away."

While Archie went in search of sherry, Lilly showed the old lady into the staff room and helped her get comfortable. A moment later, Archie was back with a tray containing a glass of sherry and a small plate of truffles topped with sugar violets.

"Oh, how lovely," exclaimed Milly.

"Compliments of Anthony," Archie explained. "He said you'd know who I meant."

"Oh, yes. He knows these are my favourites. How thoughtful of him. Now, what would you like to know?"

Lilly reviewed the notes Archie had taken while interviewing the staff.

"I understand Charlie was your original server, before a young lady called Elizabeth took over?"

"That's right. Such a shame what happened to him. It must have been an accident, but I suppose if the customer makes a complaint, then it has to be followed through. Even though the poor boy did go to apologise."

"He did?" said Archie. "When was that?"

"Not long after he was let go I think it was. He came to tell me what had happened and explained someone else would be my server for the remainder of the journey. I felt terribly sorry for him and suggested perhaps if he went to apologise to the gentleman concerned, it would make things right. He said that's where he was going."

Charlie failed to mention that, Lilly thought, making her own notes now, as well as Archie.

"Did you see anyone else coming through to this end of the train?" Archie asked.

Milly took a sip of sherry and thought for a moment.

"Bobby Smith entered and stopped to talk to me for a little while. He was quite pleasant."

"Oh, you know him?" Lilly asked.

"No, dear. He introduced himself. Asked if I was enjoying the journey, if I'd made the trip before, that sort of thing. He was just being polite and making conversation."

"And did he carry on to the end carriages?"

"I can't be sure. I was doing my crossword at the time and had a sticky cryptic clue I was trying to fathom out. I didn't even see him walk back, although I suppose he must have done."

"Was there anyone else you noticed, Milly?" Archie asked.

"Oh, of course. How stupid of me," she said, delving into her carpet bag and pulling out a book. "The author, Katherine Harp. She gave me a signed copy of her book, see? She was a sweet girl. Terribly glamorous, I thought. Do you know, I've never dared to wear bright red lipstick? It wasn't done in my day unless you wanted to get a rather unfortunate reputation. But again I can't tell you if she moved further down the train or when she came back, I'm afraid. There was one other gentleman who passed, and I believe he did leave the carriage. I don't know his name, though."

"Can you describe him?" Lilly asked.

"Oh yes, quite easily. I noticed him particularly because he was wearing a beautiful blazer, very similar to one my late husband had. Then, after he'd gone back in the direction of the other carriages and the bar, his wife came in search of him. I think she must have come back here too."

"Was she a brunette wearing a long floral dress?"

"Why, yes."

"Colin and Deborah Kimble," Archie said, and Lilly nodded.

"Just one other question," Lilly said. "Can you remember the order they went through? For example, did you see Charlie before Colin, or was it the other way around?"

"I'm not certain, I'm afraid. Time doesn't really mean much when you're on a trip like this, does it? People pass by all the time. Some you notice, some you don't. I do realise how important that question is, but I just can't be sure and I would hate to get it wrong."

"Of course," Lilly said, feeling disheartened. It would have been very useful knowing who had come last, because assuming they'd gone to the far end of the carriage; they couldn't have failed to notice a body. "Thank you so much for your time, Milly. You've been extremely helpful."

"You're welcome, my dear. If I remember anything else, I'll be sure to let you know. Now, young man," she said, smiling up at Archie. "Would you be so kind as to see me back to my seat?"

While Archie was gone, Lilly compared his notes with her own and jotted down bits she had missed from the other interviews.

"What a wonderful woman!" Archie said as he came back. "I sincerely hope I'm tootling about on trains when I'm her age. Do you know she's done some fantastic railway journeys in her time? It's only in her later years she's had to make do with the more local day trips. One of her favourites was the Trans-Siberian, but she's also done the famous Blue Train in South Africa and the Indian Palace on Wheels."

"They sound amazing, Archie. What fabulous experiences."

"We should seriously consider doing one ourselves, Lilly. What do you think?"

"Absolutely! It would be lovely to have something to look forward to. As long as there isn't a murder to solve while we're there."

Archie shuddered. "Heaven forbid. This one is bad enough. Do you think we're getting anywhere, Lilly?"

"I think so. Slowly. But we're not trying to solve it, remember? We're just trying to make as much headway as we can before the police arrive, then we can pass on what we've learned. So, back to Milly. Can we rely on her memory?"

Archie nodded. "I think we can. She's really switched on for her age. She may get the order of things a bit jumbled, which she admitted herself, but I think we can certainly take it as read that those people she mentioned could have come through to this carriage."

"All right. Well, that means we have more suspects than I thought. We need to speak to Colin and Deborah Kimble."

THEY DECIDED THE best approach this time, rather than getting Charlie to bring the Kimbles down to the interview room, would be to go in search of them and speak to them both together wherever they happened to be. Providing it wasn't too crowded. Partly to get them by surprise and partly because they were both getting a little claustrophobic and fed up with the same four walls.

They wandered back through the next first-class cabin where they found Milly with an open book on her knee, but with her eyes closed and snoring gently. Lilly had mentioned to Archie how well she had understood them, considering she was hard of hearing, and Archie had explained she'd turned up her hearing aids to their maximum setting. He also let her in on a secret Milly had shared with him. That if she found her environment too noisy, or was talking to a particular person whom she found hard work, then she would turn them down and tell them she couldn't hear. She found it a very effective way of getting rid of people she had no wish to entertain. Lilly found this little admission highly amusing.

"Oh, she's a wily old bird, and no mistake," Archie had said with much admiration.

They moved through the next carriage, which, decoration wise, was the same as the other first-class carriages, but this was much noisier, with numerous passengers chatting to their companions or across the aisles to others. Several were standing, tea and coffee cups in hand, while others had moved away from their assigned seats altogether and were socialising with people further down the train.

As they walked, several people nodded and smiled, but mostly they stared with undisguised interest. Word had naturally spread that she and Archie were investigating a serious crime. No one, however, asked them any questions, which Lilly found a bit odd, but was extremely relieved about.

The next carriage was the formal bar, a beautiful art deco inspired space, with brass and green leather stools at the lozenge shaped bar, which had fan designed, etched glass panels at the bottom and a top of green marble. The ceiling was made up of square panels with the TLE logo in the centre of each picked out in gold leaf. The soft lighting running around the entire ceiling, and the accompanying tiffany-style lamps completed the look. It was sumptuous. It was also where they found Deborah and Colin Kimble.

They were at a table seated in green leather club chairs at the far end of the space, nursing a shared pot of coffee, and as the bar was relatively quiet, most passengers opting to have their beverages served at their own or their friends' tables, it was the perfect setting for Lilly and Archie to interview them.

It was Deborah who noticed them first and nudged her husband. He turned round and grinned.

"Ah, it's the detectives. Is it our turn to be interrogated now?" he said, a little too loudly.

Lilly frowned. It appeared as though Colin was a tad drunk, even though there had been no alcohol served for quite some time. Then she spied the silver flask just visible in his blazer pocket.

She returned his smile. "Yes, actually, it is."

"Oh," Colin suddenly seemed less enthusiastic. "You're serious?"

"Don't worry, it's just a chat," Archie said, bringing two additional chairs over to the table.

"Well, I must admit," Colin said, looking around the bar and nodding. "It's the perfect setting for it. I feel as though I'm in one of those old murder mystery films. So, which one of you is the lead detective? And is it that old, good cop bad cop scenario you see in the American movies?"

Deborah giggled and lightly punched her husband's arm. "Colin, you are silly."

"You seem awfully amused considering the gravity of the situation, Mr Kimble," Archie said.

Colin laughed. "Oh, so it's Mr Kimble now, is it? What happened to Colin?"

"Are you aware of what's happened?" Lilly asked before the conversation deteriorated further.

"We're stuck on a stationary train with no way to leave. It's currently a hot-bed of rumour and Chinese whispers. Of course we know what's happened. Besides, that's what comes of interviewing Katherine first. It took her all of ten seconds to come and tell Deborah. Isn't that right, dear?"

Deborah nodded. "Yes. She couldn't help herself. She's a bit of a gossip, I'm afraid, and loves to be the first one to impart news."

"How do you know Katherine?" Lilly asked. "You both seem quite well acquainted with her."

Colin waved a hand. "That's my wife's doing. You tell her, Deborah."

"I am a huge fan of her books. I don't get much time to read, but as soon as one of her's comes out, I have to go and buy it. It's my not-so-secret vice. They're colourfully written, but that's part of their charm. And who doesn't love a good romance with a happy ever after?"

"So, presumably you know Vincent too?" Lilly asked, while Archie, once again, very kindly scribbled notes.

"Only through Katherine," Deborah replied, taking a sip of her coffee. She grimaced as she realised it had gone cold and signalled to the waiter to bring them a fresh pot.

"Tell her how you met," Colin instructed his wife.

Deborah sighed. "It was at one of her book signings. I brought my whole collection for her to sign and we got talking. I found out she was most likely going to have to stop writing because her real job, and life in general as I understood it, meant she was just too busy. Well, I couldn't bear it. I looked forward to every new book and the thought of not having any more was an awful prospect. So, I convinced Colin to sponsor her next book, meaning she was able to take some time off work and concentrate on her writing. And thank goodness she did, because her literary career has taken off exponentially as a result. We no longer sponsor her, there's no need, she is making a very good living from her books."

"It was very kind of you to become her benefactor like that," Lilly said. "And it obviously worked out well."

"Oh, yes, she's one of the most popular writers in her genre now," Colin said. "She has a talent for the type of stuff she writes. Not my thing, of course, but knowing she was writing more books kept my wife happy. Katherine's fun to have around as well. A real social butterfly who is always introducing us to new people. She's very appreciative of what we did for her and it's proven a fruitful investment on our part, too."

"Oh?" Archie said, looking up from his notes. "Why is that?"

"She has all her book launch parties at our businesses," Deborah explained. "It's her way of saying thank you, and we often get new clients and plenty of exposure as a result. We have a good relationship."

Lilly nodded. "And now I need to ask you about another of Katherine's relationships," she said. And Archie turned to a new page, trying not to smile at her clumsy attempt to segue into the next line of questioning. She kicked him under the table and cleared her throat.

"So, AM I correct in assuming you met Vincent when Katherine and he were dating?"

Colin nodded. "I was hoping to have a male writer friend like Deborah has in Katherine. They're an interesting bunch are writers. But it ended between them and things became a little awkward."

"Any idea who broke up with who?" Archie said.

"That entirely depends on who you ask," Colin chuckled. "I really have no idea. Do you, Deborah?"

"I honestly don't know. Katherine's a very proud woman. I imagine if it was Vincent who called it quits, then she wouldn't want it becoming public knowledge. She told me it was her, but Vincent sang a different tune. She likes to pretend her relationships are just a bit of frivolous fun, not serious on her part, but I truly believe she fell for Vincent. Truthfully, I didn't take to him, mainly because of how he treated her, but their personal life was nothing to do with me. The relationship didn't last long."

Lilly studied the couple for a moment. She couldn't quite read them. Normally, she was quite good at getting the measure of people. *They have the appearance of not knowing Vincent well at all, more that they knew of him. Perhaps there had been a couple of double-dates with Katherine and him, but probably nothing else.* She thought.

"What were your reasons for going to the rear of the train this evening?" she asked, eying them carefully to gauge their reactions. Neither seemed surprised at the question.

"I went back to speak to Vincent, actually," Colin said. "We obviously weren't there for his presentation at the conference, but I wanted to know if he'd got some solid interest from the publishers. While things between him and Katherine didn't end well, there was no cause for us to fall out with him."

"Speaking of his book," Deborah said in hushed tones. "Is there any chance I could have a look at it? When he and Katherine were still an item, he told me he was writing something based on a true story but with a murderous twist. I'd love to read it."

"Well, apart from that being highly unethical and morally questionable," Archie said, quite put out Lilly thought, and rightly so. "The book is missing. Most likely stolen by whoever killed him."

It was a subtle movement, but both Lilly and Archie noticed Colin shift in his seat and turn away.

"Is everything all right, Colin?" Archie asked.

"I think it's just hit home that Vincent is really dead. It's making me feel a bit uneasy and quite sick to think someone on here is responsible. That poor man. And why would someone steal his manuscript?"

"We don't know as yet," Lilly said, turning her attention to Deborah. "You never said why you went to the back of the train?"

"I was looking for Colin, actually. He told me why he wanted to talk to Vincent, but after I'd thought about it, I didn't want him to become friends with Vincent again. I know Colin will disagree with me, but it is Katherine who is our friend, and she who helps our business. Not Vincent. And more importantly, as I said before, he treated Katherine appallingly."

"Now, Deborah," Colin said. "We've had this conversation before. What went on between those two is nothing to do with us. There's no harm in being civil to the man."

"Civil is one thing, Colin, friends is another thing entirely. Anyway, it's a moot point now. The man is dead."

Colin nodded and busied himself pouring coffee, just stopping short of reaching for his flask to add some whiskey, Lilly noticed.

"Did you find Colin?" Lilly asked Deborah.

"No. A nice old lady told me I'd just missed him. He'd already been through and then come back. Obviously, there was no need to go any further. I assumed he was in the bathroom and I'd missed him that way. I was right as it happened. But he'd already used the facilities and returned to the bar. Which is where I found him. He'd ordered some bubbly, which was a lovely surprise."

"Of course I did, my dear. If we're going to be stuck on a train, we may as well make the most of it." They both chuckled. "It's a shame they've stopped serving, isn't it? We've paid good money to be on this trip. The least they can do is keep the alcohol flowing while we're stuck here."

"Oh, I know. I rather fancied one of those signature cocktails."

"I'll buy you the biggest cocktail you can drink when we go to France next month," Colin told his wife. "Get it served in a bucket!" and they both laughed.

"Make sure there's two straws," Deborah said, and they both laughed again.

Lilly glanced at Archie and raised an eyebrow. *They're both so giddy*, she thought. It didn't feel proper given the current circumstances. Neither of them appeared drunk enough to find murder amusing. It almost felt as though they were faking their carefree, nonchalant attitudes. Perhaps the marriage was rocky? Or maybe one of them killed Vincent, and they were trying to mask their fear with over-exuberance?

Colin turned back to Lilly and Archie. "So, have we finished?"

Lilly nodded. "Yes, I think that's it for now," she said, getting up.

Deborah and Colin Kimble were chatting loudly as Lilly and Archie made their way out of the bar.

"I hope they've got some of those chocolate truffles left," they heard Deborah say as they slid the carriage door closed.

"I don't know what to make of those two," Lilly said, coming to a halt between the two carriages and pulling Archie to the side where they wouldn't be seen.

"No, I don't either. They were quite amusing as lunch companions, but now, considering there has been a murder and the fact they are both worse for wear with drink, I find I don't like them very much at all."

"I think they know more than they're letting on. Did you get the feeling that was all an act just for us?"

"It was certainly a bit phony. And in very poor taste."

"I feel as though everyone so far has lied to us in some way. It's really frustrating, Archie. We'll never find out anything concrete if people are keeping things from us."

"You don't think they're all in cahoots, do you? Like the book?"

"Crikey, I hope not!" Lilly said, folding her arms and looking at the floor while she pondered the question for a moment. "No, I don't think that's what happened. Besides, if that were the case, it was stupid to pose Vincent and the crime scene the way they did. It just points at there being multiple culprits. I believe our killer was trying to send a vastly different message. But what it is, I don't know yet."

"We've interviewed those who knew Vincent and those close to the scene. What do you want to do next?"

"Look for clues."

"We've already gone over the scene."

"Yes, but we haven't looked through the suspect's bags," Lilly said. "And I know two who are currently away from their seats."

"Ah, right," Archie said, glancing back at the bar. "And this is legal, is it?"

"We've been given authority to investigate by the chap in charge of the train, so I'd say yes. If I'm wrong, then we feign ignorance."

"Oh, jolly good. But just so you know, they won't let us share a cell when we're arrested."

Chapter Nine

LILLY AND ARCHIE hurriedly made their way back to their own carriage, trying not to draw attention to themselves. As luck would have it, Deborah and Colin Kimble had been assigned the same one but at the opposite end. It meant they wouldn't look too out of place when they began to search. Not that there were any people inside, Lilly realised, looking about. It appeared everyone had got bored sitting around and ventured off en masse in search of something to do. Katherine Harp was the only one left, but she didn't even look up from the notebook she was scribbling in when they went in.

The Kimble's table was immediately on the right as they entered, and Lilly spied a brown leather briefcase on the overhead luggage rack, inscribed with the letters CK.

"Bingo," Lilly said, dragging it down.

"Just what do you think you're doing?" a furious voice snapped behind them. Deborah had just entered and caught them red-handed. She took a single stride and snatched the bag from Lilly's hands. "How dare you?" she spat. "What gives you the right to go searching through our belongings?"

"Is everything all right, Deborah?" Katherine called out as she hurried up the aisle, an unmistakable look of glee plastered on her face.

Deborah clutched the briefcase to her chest. "These two were trying to search Colin's bag! Just what were you looking for? Money?"

Lilly saw Archie look at her in amazement. "Mrs Kimble, you are aware we're investigating what happened to Vincent Wales?" he began, but she cut him off.

"I don't care what you two amateurs think you're doing," she snarled, then turned to her friend. "Katherine, go and get my husband, would you? I'm sure he'll have a thing or two to say about this."

Lilly could see Katherine was relishing all the drama as she went in search of Colin. In fact, she wouldn't be surprised if some of it ended up in Katherine's next novel.

"It's a good job I came to use the bathroom, isn't it?" Deborah said, all vestiges of the friendly personality she'd shown them earlier vanishing. "Just what was it you were trying to steal?"

"Oh, for crying out loud, you silly woman," Archie said, at the end of his tether. "We're not stealing anything. We're investigating a murder!"

"You're not the police," she snapped.

Lilly pulled Archie to one side. "I'm going to go and see Kenneth Warren. I think it's prudent to get some official back-up."

"Good idea. But I'm coming with you before I do something I regret."

"All right. And, Archie, try to stay calm. Think of your blood pressure."

Archie smiled. "Very funny. Let us go and find Kenneth."

*T*HEY FOUND KENNETH Warren in the staff lounge with Charlie.

"Ah, Miss Tweed, Mr Brown, have you found out anything?"

"We've learned quite a lot, but found nothing definitive. I'm actually hoping you can help, Mr Warren?" Lilly said. "We need to look through some of the passenger's bags and were in the process of searching Colin Kimble's when his wife turned up. She's absolutely furious with us."

"You have a suspect list?"

Lilly nodded. "I believe the killer was someone Vincent knew well. That leaves Katherine Harp, Bobby Smith, Charlie and the Kimbles. There's something important belonging to Vincent that's missing. I need to look for it."

Kenneth Warren nodded, glancing at Charlie.

"It wasn't me, Mr Warren. I swear."

"You're still a person of interest, Charlie," Lilly said. "But the sooner I can start to search, the sooner I can find out something that will help us."

"Yes, I can see that," Kenneth Warren said. "Why don't we gather that group of people together in your carriage and demand they open their luggage for inspection? I doubt any innocent party would object."

"I appreciate your help," Lilly said. "The only one missing is Bobby Smith. The others are on their way."

"Give me a couple of minutes to find him. Charlie, you go along with Miss Tweed and Mr Brown."

Charlie sighed but dutifully followed them both back to the carriage, where Deborah was still defiantly clutching her husband's bag. She shot them a venomous look. A moment later, Colin entered with Katherine and shortly after that, Kenneth Warren turned up with Bobby Smith in tow. He'd posted staff at either end of the carriage to ensure the proceedings would be conducted in private. He cleared his throat.

"If I could have your attention, please. As you are aware, there has been a serious crime committed on this train. The police are on their way, however, due to where we have stopped, it will be some time until they reach us."

Colin groaned. "Oh, that's just great. I bet it will be past midnight by the time they arrive. Then what? How long are you intending to keep us here?"

"As long as it takes for them to arrive, Mr Kimble. They are traversing on foot and as such..."

"On foot? What on earth for?"

"Because, while you obviously realise we have stopped, what you are unaware of is that we are currently sitting on the top of the viaduct, some thirty-two metres above the ground."

There was a collective gasp from everyone crowded at the end of the carriage, Lilly and Archie included. Being unable to see anything outside, they had no idea of their precarious situation.

"Now," Kenneth Warren continued. "How long we remain here when the police arrive will be down to how far our own investigations have got. You all knew the victim Vincent Wales, and because it's apparent his murder was premeditated, we've come to the conclusion the killer is most likely one of you."

"NOW WAIT JUST a minute," Colin said, at the same time as Katherine blurted out, "How dare you!" and Deborah said, "That's utter nonsense."

The only one who didn't appear to take umbrage was Bobby Smith, who laid a hand on Katherine's shoulder and said, "Calm down, Katherine. We all knew Vincent. It makes sense to be looking at all of us first."

"Precisely," Lilly said. Glad that at least one person was seeing sense. "Now, Deborah, we need to search through everyone's belongings, as I indicated earlier. And I'd like to start with that briefcase you're holding."

"I don't think so," Colin said, snatching the bag from his wife. "This contains information about private business transactions, which have nothing to do with what's going on here."

"Oh, very convenient," Charlie said. "You know that just makes you look suspicious?"

"Aren't you the one who poured hot tea on Vincent?" Bobby said to Charlie. "I don't think you should be pointing fingers, son. You're as much of a suspect as the rest of us."

"That's enough," Kenneth said. "Mr Kimble, one way or another, we are searching that bag. I'd rather it be with your consent."

Colin glared, but still held tight to his bag.

"Colin," Katherine said softly. "You're just making yourself look guilty. Why not just cooperate if you've nothing to hide?"

"I think you should," Deborah said. "They'll do it anyway."

"Fine!" Colin said and practically threw it at Lilly. Luckily, she caught it without it hitting her.

"Watch it, Colin," Archie said through clenched teeth.

Lilly opened the case on one of the tables and she and Archie went through it meticulously. There were a number of notebooks which Lilly flicked through, but nothing fell out. A planner with times and dates of various appointments. Pens and a pad of post-it notes. A number of folders containing business propositions, as Colin had said. Then, right at the bottom, a small envelope. The moment she drew it out of the bag, she saw Colin stiffen.

"What is it?"

"Nothing to do with you," he cried, about to snatch it from her hand, but Bobby Smith held him back.

"What's the matter, old chap?" he asked.

"Nothing. It's private. And get your hands off me."

Lilly opened the envelope and pulled out a sheet of paper. "It's a love letter."

"What?" Deborah said. "What do you mean, it's a love letter? Who to?"

"It was for you," Colin said. "I hadn't had the chance to give it to you yet."

"Read it," Deborah demanded.

Lilly cleared her throat.

> *To my one and only true love,*
> *The sight of you so near yet untouchable is almost more than I can bear. I long for the night when we can be in each-other's arms again and I can have you all to myself.*

"It's a tad short," Lilly said.

"I hadn't finished writing it," Colin said, stammering.

"You were writing me a love letter?" Deborah said, turning to her husband.

"I don't know," Archie said, taking the note. "It looks an awful lot like a woman wrote this. I could be wrong, of course. Deborah," he said, handing her the note. "Is this your husband's writing?"

Deborah took the letter and studied it briefly. "Yes, it could be. Colin has lovely handwriting." She looked up at him with a desperate look on her face. "You really were writing me a love letter?"

"Yes, of course I was, dear."

Lilly looked at them both and could see Deborah really wanted to believe her husband but didn't. It was obvious Colin was lying. She took the letter back and opened one of Colin's notebooks to compare. "The handwriting doesn't match at all. See?"

"I think you're wrong," Deborah shouted. "You're just trying to cause trouble. Colin writes much neater when he's trying to. The stuff in the notebooks is written at speed. More scrawls dashed off quickly than properly written. You can't possibly compare them."

"Oh, come on, Deborah, you can't honestly believe he wrote this letter?" Lilly said.

"I know my husband's handwriting and that is it! Now, I'm not discussing it anymore."

Archie gave Lilly a slight nudge and shake of his head. He obviously meant for her to drop it. She sighed. "Is there anything else in there?" she asked him as he was rummaging through a side pocket of the briefcase.

Archie pulled out a mobile phone and, turning it on, swiped the screen where a prompt for a password appeared. He looked at Colin. "Would you mind unlocking your phone?"

"Absolutely not. It contains all my client information as well as access to my stocks and shares accounts. Forget it. If the police wish to look through my phone, that's one thing, but I'm not unlocking it for you and that's final." He reached over and snatched his phone from Archie's hand. "You've already gone through my bag and found nothing. Obviously, because I have nothing to hide."

Lilly stepped around Colin and he turned in surprise. She then edged past Katherine and walked over to the writer's table, where she picked up her notebook. The one she had been scribbling in for most of the evening. "I thought so," she said and everyone moved up the aisle and gathered round. "Katherine wrote this letter. Look." She held the letter and the notebook side by side so everyone could see the writing was identical. "Can you explain this, Katherine?"

Katherine rolled her eyes. "I write love letters for all my books. I did not, however, write that one."

"Oh, come on," Charlie said. "A blind man on a galloping horse could see it's your handwriting. You must have written it."

"She didn't," Colin snapped. "And even if she did, what does it have to do with Vincent?"

"Someone is lying," Lilly said. "It's not easy to try to get to the truth when people are keeping secrets."

Katherine scowled and put her hands on her hips. She was becoming defensive. "Why don't you say what it is you're thinking? What exactly are you accusing me of?"

"All right," Lilly said, nodding. "Katherine Harp, are you and Colin Kimble having an affair?"

Colin let out a furious shout. "How dare you!" he roared. "I just told you I wrote that letter for my wife! Quit trying to play detective. You're obviously not very good at it. You're just a tea shop owner with an inflated ego."

"I've just about had enough of your insults and bad manners, Kimble," Archie shouted. "Apologise to Miss Tweed, this instant."

"I'll do no such thing, and I'll thank you to keep you beaky nose out of my business."

"That's enough," Kenneth Warren said, pushing in between Archie and Colin. "Miss Tweed, bring me the letter and the notebook, please. Let's see if we can't get to the bottom of the matter calmly and rationally."

Chapter Ten

I T TOOK KENNETH Warren longer to find his glasses than it did to declare that the writing on both the notebook and the letter were, in his opinion, a match.

"Utter nonsense!" Katherine exclaimed, pushing through the crowd at the table in an attempt to take back her notebook, but Archie stopped her.

"Just wait a moment, Ms Harp. We're trying to get to the bottom of what's going on here."

Lilly could see the atmosphere in the carriage was becoming increasingly tense and was about to try to smooth things over when Bobby Smith spoke.

"You know, looking closer, I don't actually think the writing is by the same hand. Colin says he wrote it, so why doesn't he do it again? Then we can see if he is the one who did it."

"No," Colin said. "I've already told you it's mine. I'm not going to play this ridiculous little game. It has absolutely nothing to do with what happened to Vincent."

"Why?" Archie asked. "If you're innocent, as you say, then this is the best way to prove it. Or is the letter from the other woman in your life, Colin?"

"It is my private letter to my wife. It is nothing to do with any of you, and I don't appreciate your unfounded accusations, Mr Brown." He raised a finger and pointed at Charlie. "What about him? Didn't he assault Vincent Wales? Burned the man with hot tea is what I heard."

Charlie stood, fists clenched at his sides. "You don't know what you're talking about. But if you're looking for someone who assaulted Vincent, then Bobby Smith is your man. He's having an affair with Katherine and he punched Vincent in a pub a few weeks ago."

"Calm down, Charlie," Kenneth said, putting a restraining hand on his arm.

"Why? What are you going to do, Mr Warren? Sack me? You've already done that in case you forgot." He turned to Colin. "I had nothing to do with Vincent's murder, but it's obvious you're deflecting because you're hiding something. And you," He said, turning to Katherine. "You did write that letter no matter what you say."

"You seem to be protesting a bit too much," Colin argued. "You have a motive, young man."

"Me? Rubbish! What about her?" he said, pointing at Katherine. "It makes sense it was her. Especially considering how the body was found."

Lilly sighed and exchanged frustrated glances with Archie. This was not the way she'd envisaged the investigation going. Nor the information of how the body and clues were posed to resemble one of the most popular crime fiction books ever written, shared. She found herself annoyed with Charlie for spilling the beans the way he had, but he was young, and if he was innocent, as he claimed, then he'd want the real culprit to be found. She supposed she couldn't blame him, really.

Archie shrugged as if to say, *better tell them, because if you don't, Charlie certainly will.*

COLIN RAISED A brow and looked pointedly at Lilly. "So, how was the body found?"

"There was an attempt to reenact the murder from the book Murder on the Orient Express," she said. "And considering Katherine and Vincent had a heated altercation about that very book this morning, it does look suspicious. However, anyone here could have chosen to do that. It was no secret Vincent was carrying the novel around. Someone could have seen it as an opportunity. And we haven't found the murder weapon yet. Unfortunately, that could be anywhere."

"And what is the murder weapon?" Deborah asked.

"Oh, come on, Deborah," Katherine said, tossing back her hair. "She just told you it was like the book. He was stabbed, obviously. So we're looking for a bloody knife."

"Stabbed?" Colin repeated, shocked.

"Repeatedly, yes?" Katherine said, glancing at Lilly who nodded. "Nine times, like in the book. Someone is playing games and I don't like it."

"Oh, give it a rest, Katherine," Deborah said sharply. "We all know you didn't read the book. But guess what? No one cares apart from Vincent."

"But that's the whole point," Charlie exclaimed, pointing a finger at Katherine. "She cared what he thought of her not knowing a famous book when she's a writer. In fact, I bet she cared enough to kill him when he made her look like an idiot in public."

"You were a couple at one point," Colin said. "You intimated the break up was your doing, and that you didn't really care. Is that not the truth, Katherine?"

"You've got it all wrong, Kimble," Bobby said, shaking his head.

Katherine's cheeks flushed and angry red and ugly pink blotches began to appear on her neck. She rushed forward and snatched her notebook off the table, roughly pushing Archie out of the way. She stormed back to her seat and reached up to the overhead luggage rack for her bag.

"I don't have to put up with all these insults. I'm going to the bar where I don't have to listen to all this rubbish."

She jerked her bag down, letting out a frustrated cry when the obviously open bag spilled its contents onto the seat and the floor. She knelt and hurriedly started snatching up bits of paper and notebooks, lipstick and mascara, stuffing them haphazardly into her bag.

Lilly bent to help, then stopped as she realised what she was looking at.

"This is the missing book," she said softly. She quickly picked up all the sheets and said louder. "This is Vincent's missing manuscript."

⚜

"KATHERINE!" LILLY SAID, louder.

"What? What do you want now?" she practically screamed, standing and putting her bag over her shoulder. "What is that?" she added, looking at the bundle of papers Lilly was holding, as though seeing it for the first time.

If this was an act, she was very convincing, Lilly thought. She looked genuinely surprised, but she'd already been proven to be an adept liar and more than a little dramatic, so Lilly wasn't taking her wide, innocent eyes at face value just yet.

Lilly had managed to put the pages in some semblance of order and was now staring at the title page: *Death of a Scarlet Woman by Vincent Wales.*

"Is that really Vincent's book, Lilly?" Archie said, leaning over her shoulder to get a better look.

Lilly nodded. "Yes."

"What is it?" Katherine said again, her face turning redder.

Lilly was becoming more exasperated with the writer. She appeared to have lost her ability to understand plain English.

"Katherine," she said slowly and deliberately, shaking the swathe of pages to make her point. "This is Vincent's missing manuscript. The one taken from the scene of the murder. It was in your bag. How did it get there?"

Lilly had never seen someone's face drain of colour so quickly. It was like watching traffic lights turn from red to green. Katherine looked sick.

"I... I don't know," she stammered. "I've never seen it before, I swear."

Everyone was staring at her now. Even Bobby Smith, who'd been a stoical support up to now, was giving her a quizzical look. Then he took an involuntary step back, looking at her with incredulity.

"Katherine, this is serious," Lilly said. "This manuscript was taken from Vincent immediately after he was killed. Obviously by the murderer. Unless you can give us a good explanation as to why it's in your bag..."

"I can't! I didn't put it there. Someone is trying to blame me. I didn't kill Vincent. I didn't!"

Archie stepped forward. "While I would like to believe what you're saying, I'm afraid the evidence says otherwise. You had both motive and opportunity, and now this damning document is found in your belongings. It doesn't look very good for you, Katherine."

"You aren't a policeman," Katherine countered. "And what opportunity? I wasn't anywhere near Vincent when we got back from the writer's conference."

"It doesn't take a copper to see what's going on here, Katherine," Bobby said, sadly. "And when they arrive, based on this, they are going to arrest you. I admit I never liked Vincent. He treated you badly, but to stab him to death because he broke up with you and some stupid insults?" he shook his head bewildered.

"I thought you broke up with him, Katherine?" Deborah said.

"Is that what she told you?" Bobby said. "No, Vincent broke her heart and if you know her like I do, then you know how sensitive her pride is."

"How dare you turn on me like this, Bobby Smith! I'm telling you, and everyone here, you've got it wrong. I did not kill Vincent Wales."

Kenneth Warren cleared his throat. "I think in light of what's just happened, it would be better for all concerned if you came with me, Miss Harp," he said. "A private carriage is available."

"To give me space or to keep an eye on me?" she asked, her eyes narrowing.

"Both," he said.

Katherine threw up her arms. "Fine, I'll go. I don't want to be here with these people, anyway."

Kenneth indicated the way and followed her out of the carriage toward the First-Class staff lounge. The atmosphere remained silent and tense for a moment, then people began to disperse. Charlie and Bobby found a corner together, as did the Kimbles. Both couples were leaning in, talking in hushed whispers. No doubt discussing the fact that Katherine was the one who had killed Vincent.

"Come on, Archie, we'll go back to our seats," Lilly said quietly. "I've just discovered something, and I want your advice."

"SO WHAT DO you want to ask me?" Archie said, while Lilly stowed the manuscript in her bag for safekeeping.

"That Katherine really is the most obvious choice as the killer."

"But?"

"But she never read Murder on the Orient Express. We all know that."

"She admitted she hadn't," Archie said. "She said she looked up the summary on-line."

"Exactly. And I've just done the same thing. Do you know what the first result is when you do a search on the name of that book? I'll tell you. It's the summary of the recent film adaptation. Not the big blockbuster, the other independent one which didn't do so well."

"Okay. But why does it matter? It's the same story."

"Not quite. This movie didn't include all the characters from the book," Lilly said. "It didn't quite work as a result. I think it was budget related. Anyway, I digress. The upshot is they cut some of the characters to save time and money."

"Movies leave out details from books all the time," Archie said. "A good job, actually, or they'd last for days. But why does that matter?"

"Because the big reveal is the fact there is more than one killer."

"I don't believe that's the case here, Lilly."

Lilly smiled and patted Archie's hand. "Just hear me out. In the book, as well as the movie, it's revealed all the characters had a connection to the victim, and they all took turns to stab him. One stab wound for each suspect."

"With you so far," Archie said with a smirk. "I have read the book several times, you know? Although I admit I can't remember some of the details."

"Sorry, Archie. But in this film, because not all the characters were included, the victim had fewer stab wounds than he did in the book. When we confronted Katherine before, she said, and I quote, 'nine times like in the book.'"

"So?"

"Archie, that's not what happened in the book," Lilly exclaimed, realising she was raising her voice. She quickly glanced over at the Kimbles, Bobby, and Charlie, but luckily, none of them had heard her. She lowered her tone and leaned toward Archie. "It's how the movie was done because they cut some of the characters. Fewer murderers mean fewer stab wounds. When Katherine looked up the on-line summary, she got the one of the indie movie, which meant *nine* stab wounds instead of the twelve that were in the book."

"And Vincent had twelve stab wounds," Archie said, nodding as he realised what Lilly was getting at. "I counted them myself."

"Exactly. So if Katherine killed and stabbed Vincent and chose to reenact the book, she would only have stabbed him nine times because that's how she believed it was originally written."

Archie sat back and stared at the ceiling. Lilly let him think and ruminate on what she'd just said.

"So, what do you think?" she said after a few minutes, in which she wondered if he'd fallen asleep with his eyes open.

"Honestly? I wonder if it's a bit of a stretch. I'm playing devil's advocate here, obviously, but she could have simply misspoken. Or could have intentionally said nine in the hope someone else would have caught the error and corrected her by saying twelve, thereby pointing the finger at them."

Lilly pulled at her lip and nodded. "Yes, that's possible too."

"Lilly, if you think something is a bit off, then we need to continue investigating. I'm with you all the way. And I don't believe we're anywhere near ready to hand our findings over to the police when they arrive. Not least because we haven't even found the murder weapon yet. I think you're right actually," He said, giving it some more thought. "There is more to this story."

Lilly nodded. "I think we're definitely missing some key element. We just need to work out what it is."

"Well, let's just hope whoever killed Vincent didn't throw the weapon out of the train window."

Chapter Eleven

LILLY HAD TO admit she wasn't feeling overly confident that Katherine was the one who had killed Vincent, it all seemed to convenient, but the evidence so far seemed to point in her direction and she had no choice but to follow the clues and evidence in front of her. Katherine was clearly referencing a film as opposed to the original book, but was it enough to absolve her of the crime? She could be very cleverly concealing the fact she had read the end of the book first, the part where Poirot reveals what happened, and mentioned nine stab wounds in order to throw Lilly off the scent. But if that was the case, what was she doing with Vincent's manuscript in her bag? She gave a sigh of frustration. She was going round in circles. Perhaps Milly could shed some additional light on the investigation? She was the only one who had both given her something definitive to work with and hadn't lied to her.

She found the elderly lady busy knitting, very aptly looking remarkably like Miss Marple, her needles clacking vigorously while she gazed around her. Lilly was always amazed that experienced knitters had no need to look at what they were doing, yet there never seemed to be any mistakes. The item just seemed to grow in front of your eyes, looking perfect. Milly had also ordered a pot of tea.

"Hello, Milly."

"Oh, hello, Lilly," she chuckled. "Milly and Lilly, we sound like a stage act, don't we? I can see us now entertaining royalty at the London Palladium. What would we be do you think? Perhaps jugglers? Or better still, unicyclists. Yes, that sounds much more exciting."

"Or jugglers on unicycles," Lilly said, smiling indulgently. The old lady's exuberance was infectious.

"Now, that sounds like a much better idea. Sit down, dear, and tell me how I can help?"

Lilly sat and took out her notebook. "I wanted to follow up on what we talked about earlier. You said you saw Mr and Mrs Kimble, Bobby Smith, Charlie, and Katherine all come through here. But you couldn't say for certain whether Katherine went through to the rear carriage. Is that right?"

Milly laid her knitting on her knee while she thought. "It's a bit of a muddle, I'm afraid. Time seems to stand still on a train. It's the oddest thing, isn't it considering we're moving at such speed? Well, most of the time anyway. Let me see. I did speak to Katherine briefly. She signed her book for me."

"I don't suppose you remember what time that was, do you?" Lilly asked, pen poised.

"It was just before dinner. I'd finished a glass of sherry and needed to pay a visit to the bathroom. Oh," she suddenly said, looking at Lilly with wide eyes. "Oh, my goodness, I think I've made a mistake. We met in the carriage outside the bathroom. Not here. She was just coming out, having used the facilities when I arrived."

"Did you see which direction she took afterwards?"

"Not exactly. I assumed she came straight back through here, because by the time I returned she was just leaving that way," she said, pointing to the door behind Lilly which led to the next first class carriage. "I thought she must have stopped to talk to someone on the way through."

"So, she could have entered the rear carriage while you were in the bathroom?" Lilly said, taking notes. "And you said you saw her just before dinner. That's when we think Vincent was killed because he was seen alive not too long prior. It was a member of the staff who came to take his dinner order who found him dead."

"Oh, my," Milly said.

"**E**XCUSE ME."

Lilly looked up to find a man with a crooked ginger moustache standing just behind her left shoulder, looking a little embarrassed. She vaguely recognised him as someone she'd spoken to not long after she and Archie had interviewed Charlie.

"Yes, can I help?" she said.

"You're investigating the death of one of the passengers? I don't know if you remember, but you spoke to me earlier. The name is Barney Waterson."

"Yes, Mr Waterson, I remember. Is there something you need to add to what you told me?"

"Not add as such. More something I failed to mention first time around," he said, shifting his weight from foot to foot.

Lilly flipped back her notebook to the relevant page and found her notes on their conversation. "You said you were in the bar until your server came to tell you dinner was served, so you returned to your seat."

"Look, I understand Miss Harp is under suspicion, and I want to set the record straight. She didn't go into the rear carriage where the body is, because she was with me at the time he is supposed to have been killed."

"With you?" Lilly said. "What were you doing?"

The man blushed beet red and Lilly realised what he was about to tell her. *Good grief, is there any red-blooded male aboard this train whom Katherine hasn't had a dalliance with?* How could she not have been aware of this man? Lilly didn't remember anyone mentioning him at all. Vincent had avoided Bobby because he was obviously aware Katherine and Bobby were close. Well, more than close, considering what she herself had witnessed in the bathroom. But Barney had just appeared out of nowhere. She wondered if he and Katherine had some history. How long had they known one another? She was about to ask that very question when Barney answered it unprompted.

"I just met her on the train this evening. I know what you're thinking, and I admit it's completely out of character for me. But Katherine is special. There was a connection right away. I can't explain it."

"Why are you coming forward now?" Lilly said. She was more than a little sceptical at the coincidence. Barney was obviously smitten with Katherine. Would he do anything, including lie to give her an alibi, in order to save her?

"Because it's my duty to tell you the truth. She's innocent and I can't, in all good conscience, let her fall under suspicion when I can prove she didn't do it."

Lilly nodded. "All right, Mr Waterson, thank you for coming forward. I think I need to have another conversation with Katherine."

Barney nodded, still blushing, and sheepishly hurried back to his seat, avoiding eye contact with the other passengers, many who had overheard the conversation and were immediately jumping to conclusions about Barney's moral character. Not to mention that of Katherine, who to anyone's ears was beginning to sound more and more like a Scarlet woman.

She said her thanks to Milly, whose eyes were sparkling with mischief and amusement at Barney's confession, and made her way back to the staff room, noting en route that Archie wasn't at their table. She'd hoped he would accompany her to see Katherine, but it didn't matter. She'd bring him up to date later.

*L*ILLY STRODE INTO the last but one carriage, determination etched on her face. Katherine was adept at bending the truth and Lilly was adamant this time she was going to get answers to her questions.

The guard on the door smiled and opened the door for her. Lilly took a deep breath and entered.

Katherine looked up from the notebook she'd been scribbling in and frowned. "What do you want?"

Lilly sat down, smoothed her trousers, crossed her legs and looked the writer in the eye. "I want to ask you about Barney."

Katherine shook her head. "Who?"

"The man you were *with* this evening."

"Don't you mean Bobby?" then she laughed. "Oh, wait. You mean the one with the lopsided moustache?"

Lilly shook her head in amazement. Katherine couldn't even remember the man's name. She wasn't a prude, but first Vincent, then Bobby, then this Barney fellow. Two different men on the same day on the same train. It was excessive in anyone's eyes.

Katherine waved a hand airily. "I don't believe I caught his name." Lilly winced and Katherine narrowed her eyes. "I don't like how you're judging me, Miss Tweed."

"Well, I apologise if I've hurt your feelings, *Miss Harp*," Lilly replied sarcastically. "But I need some truthful answers from you. There's a man dead in the next carriage. A man you were in a relationship with. Now I find you've had assignations with two other men on this train, and from what I understand, you hardly know either of them."

"It's research!" Katherine exclaimed, and Lilly had to fight the urge to roll her eyes. "Look, Lilly," Katherine said, her tone switching to reasonable like a flipped switch. "A girl has to have some fun experiences to write about if she's to put out as many romance books as I do. And we did have fun. Me and... what was his name again? Barney?"

Lilly nodded. "Luckily for you, Barney has said you were with him and didn't go to the rear carriage."

Katherine flipped her hair over her shoulder. "So, you know I'm innocent, then?"

Lilly sighed to herself. She knew Katherine was the sort of person who would relish the publicity that would come from the notoriety of being unjustly accused of murdering a former lover. She could see a circuit of radio shows and local television appearances on the horizon, no doubt blaming Lilly for the wrongful accusations. But, if Katherine wasn't guilty, then Lilly had a long night ahead of her to try to find out who was.

Lilly brought herself back to the present and said, "It doesn't matter what I think. It's what I can prove. And as Barney Waterson has just given you an alibi, I obviously need to look elsewhere."

"Well, I'm glad you're eventually beginning to see sense and starting to look for the real murderer, Lilly."

Lilly was saved from replying when the door opened and Archie walked in.

"Lilly, can I have a word?" he said, beckoning.

"Yes, of course. Katherine, thank you for your time. I'll leave you to your writing and research."

Out in the corridor, Archie took her elbow and steered her out of the hearing of the guard.

"What is it, Archie?"

"I found it," he whispered. "I've found the murder weapon."

Chapter Twelve

ARCHIE SLID THE door open from the carriage and entered the small connecting corridor, which linked to the next carriage along. The one where Milly was seated. Like the rest of the train, no expense had been spared on the interior fittings of these joined areas, and there was a plush carpet beneath their feet.

"Look here," Archie said, pointing to a dim corner where there was a bump. "I almost didn't see it because of the low wattage lighting. But it's definitely there."

Lilly couldn't believe it. Archie had found the murder weapon right outside the carriage where the bathroo-m and the first-class staff lounge were. The carriage everyone had access to. She and Archie must have walked by the weapon at least five times since they'd started the investigation. It made sense that the murderer had had to hide the weapon immediately after the murder, but Lilly could have kicked herself for not thinking to look here sooner. Hopefully, it would provide some additional clue to who had killed Vincent.

"Well done, Archie. Thank goodness they didn't throw it from the window."

"Apparently these connecting windows and doors are all locked when the train is in motion to prevent people falling. Or jumping out, I suppose. It could have been their first idea, but when they discovered it wasn't possible, whoever it was did the only thing they could. They certainly thought on their feet. There's no doubt about that."

"They must have worked incredibly quickly. They could have been disturbed at any time by someone visiting the bathroom. The panic and the rush of adrenaline must have been enough to keep them going, but they were very lucky. However, did you find it?"

"I was looking out of the window to see if I could see any sign of the police arriving, and would you believe I trod on it? The carpet at the edge has been cut, probably by the weapon itself, to allow it to be slid underneath and hidden. It would have only taken seconds to achieve."

Lilly bent down and carefully pulled up the side of the carpet closest to the wall, and there it was, a large steak knife, the wickedly sharp looking blade covered in blood.

"Archie, we need a bag to put it in. We can't let anyone handle it as there might be fingerprints the police can take from it."

"I'll go and see what I can find."

Moments later, he returned with a large transparent plastic bag, with a self-seal strip, from the kitchen and handed it to Lilly.

"I need to pick it up without touching it," Lilly mused.

"I thought of that," Archie said, flourishing a pair of heavy silver sugar tongs.

"Brilliant, Archie, these are perfect," Lilly replied, lifting the knife by the tip of the blade and lowering it into the bag. She closed the seal and handed it and the tongs back to Archie.

"I was thinking perhaps we should deposit this safely in the carriage with the body ready for the police," Archie said. "What do you think?"

"I was going to suggest that myself."

On the way, Lilly asked the staff member guarding Katherine if he could arrange for cups of green tea for the two of them? He nodded, saying they had several types and which would she prefer? She chose lemon and ginseng and thanked him. She also asked him not to mention what they'd discovered, as it could impede the investigation. Lilly had seen him surreptitiously watching from where he was standing guard. He gave her his word.

Archie unlocked the door with the key Kenneth Warren had given them, and with a deep breath each they entered. Not long after, they stood with their backs against the closed door sipping green tea.

"This is good for brain health," Lilly said. "And goodness knows we need all the help we can get at the moment."

"I can't believe I'm drinking green tea in the middle of a crime scene," Archie said with a grimace. "This is about as far from the romantic trip I had planned as it gets."

"Don't worry; we have plenty of time for future trips, Archie. Although this will be one we won't forget in a hurry."

"You can say that again. So, let's talk it through. What about suspects? My money is still on Katherine Harp. Everything so far points to her. Her stories aren't consistent and she had means and motive. She had a volatile relationship with the victim, and his manuscript, which was written about her in a very unfavourable way, was found in her bag."

Lilly realised, in the excitement of finding the knife, she hadn't told Archie about Barney. "All that's true, but unfortunately, she now has an alibi."

"What? What alibi?"

Lilly told her about the conversation with Milly, how Barney had interrupted them and what he had admitted to. "If he's telling the truth, then it would have been impossible for Katherine to murder Vincent."

"*If* he's telling the truth," Archie emphasised. "Miss Harp is obviously promiscuous and from you've just said this Barney fellow is obviously very taken with her. He could very easily have fabricated an alibi, not believing her guilty because of his feelings for her. Or Katherine could have persuaded him to vouch for her for the same reason."

"I suppose it's possible, Archie, but I find it hard to believe he'd voluntarily become an accomplice to murder, or at the very least complicit in subverting the course of justice, purely because he was enamoured with a pretty face and sexual favours from someone he's literally just met. Why would he take such a risk?"

"She's certainly making herself available to an awful lot of men, Lilly. She could have a number of people spinning her version of events and we wouldn't know it."

Lilly knew what Archie said was right. Katherine had been the first person they had spoken to, and although they had told her to keep quiet, she'd gone back out and blabbed about what she'd learned to Deborah. She could easily have talked to Bobby and both the Kimbles before she and Archie had had a chance to, and spun a tale that made her look innocent. Stories were her stock-in-trade, after all. Then she remembered Bobby had told them Katherine was talking about the case before he was interviewed.

"She certainly couldn't wait to tell people about the murder. But let's keep her on hold for the minute. Her confusion over how many times he was stabbed is still bothering me. We'll also need to talk to Bobby Smith again."

"I agree. The thing that makes Bobby a viable suspect is how violent the attack was. And he ended up in a pub fight with Vincent over a woman he hardly knew. That speaks volumes as to his nature, if you ask me."

"But he was defending her, Archie. Vincent had treated her appallingly."

"I know, but when does resorting to physical violence ever solve anything? What happened to verbal assaults? Cut your man down with a quick-witted retort or two, that's what I say."

"Yes, but you're a wordsmith, Archie. I doubt Bobby would have stood a chance against Vincent when it came to clever linguistic insults."

"I thought you were against violence?"

"I am. And I agree Bobby could have handled it better. All I'm saying is, he did the best he could, given his limitations. That doesn't mean he's not a suspect. He's one as much as the rest of them."

"Absolutely. The way Vincent was strangled to death supports that. I would imagine you'd need a good deal of strength to kill someone in that way, especially when they would be fighting back."

"What makes you think he died of strangulation and not the stabbing?"

"His wounds," Archie said. "If he was stabbed first, there would be a lot more blood because his heart would still be pumping. But look, there isn't," he said, gesturing to the far end of the carriage where Vincent's body lay. "It's far too clean a crime scene for him to have been stabbed first."

Lilly gazed up at her friend in admiration. She realised his years as an investigative crime reporter had turned Archie into the perfect murder solving partner.

"And that's like the book too," she said. "Although the victim was poisoned as opposed to strangled first. The other suspects are Charlie, Deborah and Colin. According to Milly, they all ventured back here at the right time."

"What do you think of Colin, Lilly?" Archie said, taking the last mouthful of tea and resting the cup and saucer on a nearby bain-marie. "That love letter was extremely odd."

"That love letter was obviously written by Katherine, whether those two want to admit it or not. But, honestly, what would that have to do with Vincent Wales?"

"There's some sort of connection we're missing here. Colin and Deborah's only link to Vincent is Katherine, correct?"

"It appears so," Lilly said, nodding. "But there's one thing I'm almost certain of. Whether Katherine is our killer or not, and I'm beginning to think she's actually innocent of the murder, she is somehow at the centre of this whole thing."

N THE CORRIDOR, Lilly approached the staff room.

"Where are you going?" Archie asked. "I thought we were going back to speak with Bobby Smith?"

"I just want to put my mind at ease about Katherine. There's something, a sixth sense, a hunch, or whatever you want to call it, telling me that while she's guilty of lax moral judgment, she's innocent of murder. I just want to see if I can confirm it."

"Lax moral judgment is very polite," Archie said with a grin.

"She says it's research for her books."

"Good grief. I think I'm in the wrong job. Perhaps I should write a book."

"Archie!"

Archie laughed and leaned over, unexpectedly kissing the top of her head, which caused her heart to flutter.

"Just a joke. All right, let's get this over with. After you," Archie said, opening the door.

Katherine rolled her eyes when Lilly and Archie entered. She was sprawled out on a sofa, notebook abandoned, looking extremely bored. The woman was a social butterfly, thriving on being the centre of attention. This forced incarceration must be tantamount to torture.

"Oh, what now?" she said wearily. "Have the police arrived to arrest me for something I didn't do?"

"Tell me why the train stopped," Lilly said.

Katherine sat up. "Because there was a murder?" she replied, voice heavy with sarcasm.

"Not this train, the one in the book. Murder on the Orient Express, how does the train come to a stop?"

Katherine stared at her. "You know I didn't read the book. I believe I've been well and truly exposed regarding that, haven't I?"

"I know, Katherine, and I'm not here to judge. Whether you read the book or not is of no concern to me. It's just one simple question, then I'll leave you alone. How did the train come to a stop in the book? You read the synopsis on-line."

"It derailed. Happy now? I can't see how this helps, Lilly."

Lilly smiled. "I'm now coming to believe you are innocent of the murder, Katherine. That's how it helps."

"I'm sorry?" she replied in confusion.

"You read the on-line synopsis for the indie movie, not the book. There are some subtle differences. The fact you mentioned Vincent had been stabbed nine times set my internal alarm bell ringing. That's how it was in the film. In the book it was twelve times. Neither did the train derail. It was stopped by heavy snowfall."

Lilly was surprised at the reaction. She'd assumed Katherine would be pleased at having been proved innocent, but instead she glared at Lilly with contempt.

"And now you're making fun of me, too?"

Lilly saw the starts of shimmering tears. Katherine obviously needed someone to set her straight. She was a woman who had everything going for her but was unable to appreciate it because of the way she'd been treated in the past. She surmised Vincent wasn't the only one who'd put her down, and a continuing barrage of insults and being talked down to must have knocked what little confidence she had in herself. It was cruel and abusive and most likely the cause of her promiscuity. She was using what she thought were her main assets to make herself feel wanted and loved, and more importantly, on an equal footing. Lilly began to feel very sorry for Katherine. What she really needed was a boost in confidence from a peer, one who wanted nothing from her. She needed to put on her Agony Aunt hat.

"Look, Katherine, I'm going to be brutally honest here. I might say some things which you don't agree with, or perceive as an insult, but they are not meant that way."

Katherine huffed in annoyance. "I don't have to listen to you."

"No, you don't," Archie said from the door where he'd been leaning ever since they'd entered. "But I would advise you to do so. Lilly will give you excellent advice. I've known her for years and while she was acknowledged as an agony aunt, she was far more than that. Although not officially qualified, she was, to all intents and purposes, an excellent therapist. She has helped a lot of people, Katherine. Why not let her help you?"

"You would say that. You're a couple."

Lilly and Archie exchanged smiles and Lilly nodded. It was true, they were a couple. She turned back to Katherine.

"It's very early days, but yes, we are. However, we've known one another for far longer than we've been together. Archie spoke the truth, Katherine. I've helped a number of people and if you'll let me, I can help you put things in perspective too. It strikes me that you've been badly treated in the past. Possibly in the distant past, but obviously more recently by Vincent Wales. But let's look at it from another angle. Vincent hadn't even published anything, yet he took every opportunity he could to belittle both you and your writing. That speaks more of the type of person he was than of you. It strikes me that he was jealous of your success. The fact is, you've been smart enough to find a niche in the market and have tapped into it. If your promiscuity is due to a misguided need to feel like you belong, then honestly, you should stop. There's no need for you to flaunt yourself so blatantly. You're attractive, vibrant, and obviously talented if your book sales and fans are anything to go by. You don't need to prove it; it's there for everyone to see. And if they can't, then they are not the sort of people you need in your life. You need to surround yourself with those who will lift you up, Katherine. Those who genuinely want you to succeed and will help you do it. Not people who will drag you down just to make them feel better about themselves and their own inadequacies. Those sorts of people are toxic and will never be true friends. You should be very proud of what you've achieved. Don't let others dictate how you should lead your life or what you write. Be kind to those who genuinely want to help and move away from those who don't. Stop the lying and the subterfuge. Be true to yourself. You'll find your life improves tremendously as a result, I guarantee it."

Katherine took out a tissue and dabbed her eyes with a shaky hand. "Wow," she said softly, looking at Archie. "You're right, she is good," she turned back to Lilly, taking a deep breath and pulling herself together. "So, what else can I tell you? I didn't kill Vincent, so what's left?"

"Is there anyone on this train who dislikes you enough to try to incriminate you? Because I'm beginning to think that's what's going on here. Whether you like it or not, you are the linchpin, the one key element at the centre of this whole affair. So, who would be clever enough to stage a murder so it points to you as the killer?"

Katherine shrugged. "The only person on this train who I know didn't like me is dead. I don't know anyone else who would do something so awful."

Lilly sighed. She knew in her gut Katherine wasn't telling her everything, but she also knew she wouldn't get anything else from her. Now she'd looked closely, she could see the emotional pain behind Katherine's eyes. For all her 'devil-may-care' attitude, Vincent's insults and slights had definitely hit their mark.

She and Archie left her patching up her ruined make-up. Archie returned to their seats to begin writing up their notes properly for when the police arrived, while she went in search of someone else to speak to. She was missing something important, but couldn't work out what it was. The only way she knew to move the investigation forward was to shake the tree and see what fell.

And the name of her first tree was Barney Waterson.

ON THE CARRIAGE she saw Milly had fallen asleep, her head leaning against the window curtain. Someone had moved her knitting to the table and put a soft wool blanket over her knees. She didn't wake her, instead moved directly to Barney's table, where she found him doing a crossword puzzle. He looked up anxiously when she sat across from him.

"Barney, can you confirm the time when you were busy with Katherine?" she asked quietly.

"I don't want to discuss it anymore."

"It's very important I get the details correct. You are her alibi, and..." Lilly stopped speaking as she noticed a wedding ring on Barney's hand. She was sure he hadn't been wearing one when she's spoken to him previously.

He covered his hand. "I removed it before I came to speak with you," he admitted.

"I see," Lilly said, trying not to sound judgmental.

"It was all a mistake. A horrible, horrible mistake. I don't know what came over me. It was like a siren call or something. The guilt has been eating away at me ever since. I love my wife and I swear, I have never done anything like this before. I intended to keep quiet, but when I knew Katherine was being accused of a murder that happened at the same time we were together, I had to come forward. I would have had it on my conscience for the rest of my life if she'd gone to prison for something I know she couldn't possibly have done. She was with me for some time before and up to when dinner was served."

"Did she mention or talk about Vincent at all?"

Barney nodded slowly. "Yes, she did say something about him, actually."

"What was it?" Lilly said, leaning forward.

"She was laughing at something that had gone wrong for him at the conference. He was supposed to have some sort of big presentation or something to a lot of publishers, but there was a change in the schedule and he ended up only talking to two or three."

This was new information to Lilly. "Why the change? Do you know?"

"Something to do with her sponsors, I think."

"Katherine's sponsors? You mean the Kimbles?"

Barney nodded. "That's them. Apparently the husband had it re-arranged."

"And you don't know why he did that?"

"I've no idea. I don't think Katherine does either. She was just highly amused at how angry Vincent was when he realised what had happened. That's all I know."

Lilly nodded and rose. "Thank you, Barney. Perhaps I could give you a word of advice? Don't wait for news of your dalliance with Katherine to reach the ears of your wife via a rumour or a third party. This sort of thing has a nasty habit of coming out regardless, and when you least expect it. It would be better for both you and your wife, and your future relationship, if you tell her yourself. And soon."

Barney frowned. "You know nothing about my relationship with my wife."

"No, I don't. But if you don't tell the truth, then your marriage could be over before you know it. It's just friendly advice, Barney. Whether you take it is up to you." Lilly said, and left.

So, Colin nearly ruined Vincent's chance of presenting to the main publishers. But why? Lilly thought. There was only one way to find out.

Chapter Thirteen

BEFORE GOING TO speak to Colin, Lilly walked past them, ignoring their questioning looks, and strode further down the carriage to Archie to share the nugget of information Barney had given her. Bobby, Charlie, and the Kimbles were all still ensconced in the one carriage, with a member of staff guarding both exits.

"It's interesting, isn't it?" Archie said, quietly so as not to be overheard. "That the Kimbles, when we had lunch with them, said they weren't going to the writer's conference, but instead were looking at possible businesses for sale for Deborah. Now, not only do we find they did attend, but they sponsor one of the main writers in Katherine, and Colin had enough clout to be able to change the schedule at a moment's notice. What is this all about?"

"I have no idea, Archie. But I'm on my way to talk to Colin now. It could be something as simple as they decided to attend briefly to support Katherine, but also to look for business premises at the same time. Then Colin decided to muck up Vincent's chances, either as a joke or in defence of Katherine. Kill two or three birds with one stone, as it were."

"Nice choice of phrase there, Lilly," Archie said, grinning.

Lilly grimaced. "Totally unintentional. Anyway, do you want to come with me? Colin set Vincent up for a fall and I want to know why."

"I do indeed. My notes are almost complete, anyway."

At the Kimble's table, Lilly and Archie stopped.

"Colin, might I borrow you for a moment?"

Colin folded his arms, frowning. "You're making enemies all over this train, you know."

Deborah leaned over and patted his arm. Lilly noticed she was flushed and slurring her words slightly. Colin's whiskey flask was on the table in front of her, protruding from beneath a napkin. She'd obviously bribed one of the staff members to keep supplying her with alcohol.

"I believe you, darling. I know you wrote that letter to me. But there's no sense in not cooperating. Just go with her and see what she has to say."

"Thank you, sweetheart," he said with a weary sigh, peeling himself from his seat. "All right, what do you want, Miss Tweed?"

"It would be better if we speak privately," Lilly said, and he reluctantly agreed.

Archie lead the way, with Colin following and Lilly bringing up the rear. She turned briefly to look at Deborah. She was staring glassy eyed at her reflection in the darkened window, but seeing nothing. Lilly wondered what thoughts were going through her mind?

Archie took them to a table for four directly opposite their own and indicated Colin should sit.

"You're very lucky my wife is so understanding," Colin said as they sat opposite. "If she, for one moment, believed your lies about that letter, then we would be having a very different conversation and you would be hearing from my solicitor forthwith."

Lilly couldn't believe what she was hearing and was about to say as much when Archie beat her to it.

"Oh, for goodness sake, pipe down, Colin. No one is fooled by your blustering. It's obvious Katherine wrote that letter and your wife is in denial. But that's not why we are here. We're trying to get to the bottom of what happened to Vincent Wales."

"I don't have to sit here and talk to you, you know. You might want to change your tune," Colin warned.

Lilly held up both hands to halt the growing animosity between the two men. "Please, just stop. This isn't getting us any further forward. Colin, we have some new information which I'd like to ask you about."

Colin glared at Archie for a moment, then turned his gaze to her. "Fine. What's your question?"

Lilly could tell Colin's anger was barely being kept in check. He was extremely defensive and looked as though he could blow his top at any minute. He wasn't going to like what she had to ask, but she found she no longer cared about his feelings. She had a murder to solve, and she was going to do her utmost to find out, once and for all, who did it.

"Tell me about your involvement with the writer's conference. We have it on good authority that you were responsible for changing the time of Vincent's presentation schedule, possibly by bribery in some form or other, so the chances of him picking up a publisher for his book were greatly reduced."

Colin slammed both of his fists down hard on the table, causing the uncollected cups to rattle in their saucers. But Lilly had been expecting his outburst and remained stoic and unmoved. Her intense, unwavering stare was clearly not what Colin had expected. Like Archie had said, he was all bluster. He lowered his hands.

"You've obviously had to resort to making things up now," was all he said.

Lilly smiled, which annoyed Colin even more, but she'd got the measure of the man. He was nothing more than a coward and a bully, and she was too strong and confident to let his tactics affect her.

"And what possible motive would I have for making it up?"

"To make yourself look good, of course. Why else?"

"Oh, Colin." Lilly shook her head. "I have no need to lie. I think you're confusing me with someone else," she said pointedly. It was a childish retort, but she was fed up with listening to his imperious nonsense and posturing. Colin blushed furiously, and Archie chuckled. "So why did you do it?" she asked again.

"I didn't. Someone is obviously making a mockery of your investigation and trying to pin the blame on me. Why would I care how many publishers were interested in Vincent's book?"

"I don't know, Colin, but you're not exactly being candid here, are you?"

"I'm being as candid as I can be with someone who is just throwing accusation after accusation at me, in the vague and misguided hope something will stick," he said.

"That's not how Lilly works, Colin," Archie said. "We've been told from another source that you interfered with Vincent's chances of obtaining a publisher. Lilly is now giving you a chance to tell your side of the story."

"Well, I already have. I'm telling you I have no reason to care how well Wales's book did; ergo I didn't interfere in his presentation. Someone is telling you fibs, and I'd like to know who?"

Lilly had no intention of giving Colin Barney's name. The anger was rolling off him in waves and she wouldn't put it past him to go in search of the man and start a brawl. That was the last thing she needed in the middle of a murder investigation. But she also had a feeling Colin was using diversionary tactics to get her and Archie to look elsewhere. What was he hiding?

"No, I'm not going to do that, Colin."

"Then we're done here," he said, and left.

"I REALLY DO NOT like that man," Archie said.

"Are you all right, Archie?"

He put an arm round her shoulders and drew her close. "I'm a bit fed up with everyone lying to us, if I'm being honest. We're never going to get to the bottom of this infernal case, Lilly. I don't know how you do it. I'm on the verge of banging people's heads together. Linguistic insults be damned!"

Lilly laughed. "Between you and me, so am I. Especially Colin and Deborah Kimble. I can't come up with a solid motive for either of them to kill Vincent, and they probably didn't, but I tell you this much, Colin is hiding something."

"Fancy a cappuccino? I need a jolt of caffeine to keep me awake. I really hope the police arrive soon. It feels like we've been stuck on this blasted train for hours."

"Thanks, Archie, coffee is a good idea," Lilly replied, stifling a yawn.

While she waited for Archie to return, she leaned against the back of the chair and closed her eyes. Perhaps if she rested for a moment, she'd begin to see things more clearly.

Lilly awoke with a start as Archie rattled his cup on the saucer.

"Sorry, I didn't mean to wake you."

"Oh, I can't believe I fell asleep. How long was I out?"

"Long enough for me to bring back the coffees and drink them both," Archie said. "And I hardly noticed the snoring at all."

"Oh no, Archie. Are you kidding?" Lilly said, mortified.

Archie laughed. "Of course I am. It was more like little snuffles. Quite endearing, actually."

"Good grief," she said, putting her head in her hands. "Why didn't you wake me?"

"You looked as though you needed it, so I left you. Do you want me to go and get you another coffee?"

Lilly shook her head. "Not coffee. I think tea would be best. Peppermint if they have it. Sorry, Archie, do you mind?"

"Of course not. Back in two shakes of a lamb's tail."

"So, have we actually learned anything?" Archie asked when he returned with her tea.

"Frustratingly, no, I don't think we have, really. Except that no one is willing to tell us the truth. Apart from Barney's information about Vincent's book pitch. I think that's too specific for him to have made up. But, I've been thinking. In Agatha Christie's book, it turns out that the victim's criminal past was his undoing. Maybe we've been looking at this from the wrong direction by concentrating on the people Vincent knew. Perhaps we should have been focused on his background instead?"

"Not a bad idea at all," Archie said. "Let's see what we can find out about Mr Wales, shall we?"

Chapter Fourteen

FOR THE NEXT hour, Lilly turned to the internet for her detective work. The signal strength was sporadic, which was a little frustrating, but the Wi-Fi was free so she couldn't complain. She'd already mentally slapped herself for not thinking of it sooner. By researching the victim, she hoped to gain a new perspective on the case to help find another avenue to investigate.

Archie sat across from her, also deeply into the research on his own phone. Surely between the two of them, they'd come up with something? Archie, as an investigative crime reporter, had more than a little experience, but usually he was coming at a murder inquiry from a different angle, and he was finding it frustrating being in the middle of a case where the culprit still needed to be identified.

"I'm looking at all these stories Vincent has posted on his blog," Lilly said. "Have you read them?" Archie looked up and shook his head. "It's the same thing he did to Charlie. Takes a picture of someone he meets, chats to them about their job or family, even their hobbies, then goes on to write some outlandish story about them. He's lucky he's never been sued."

"I certainly wouldn't call being murdered a better alternative," Archie said.

"Obviously. But do you think his death could have something to do with one of these stories?"

"We already have Charlie as a person of interest, Lilly. I read the story Vincent wrote about him, and I can see why he went through such a rough time with it. But Charlie said none of it was true, correct?"

"Yes, but on the blog, Vincent said it was based on a true story. I'd be absolutely livid if it was me. No wonder Charlie took it so badly. It made a complete mess of his life for a while until he could prove he was innocent of everything Vincent accused him of."

Archie loaded the blog on his phone and spent a moment reading through the links. "You're right. It looks as though Vincent had a habit of writing controversial posts on-line."

They spent a while reading the stories and looking at the accompanying photos, even taking time to read all the comments at the bottom, but while there were several from irate people threatening to get legal advice, none, apart from Charlie, seemed to be linked to anyone else who was on the train with them.

Then Lilly remembered that Katherine had mentioned how she did her research. Had Vincent done something similar? But how would she find out if he had?

"Other than a plethora of dubiously written stories, I can't find anything suspect on him at all. What about you?"

"Same," Archie said, putting down his phone and rubbing his eyes. "I've tapped into some of my networks and he's never been arrested as far as I can see. His past seems to be clean. I honestly thought we were on the right track and that we'd drum up something interesting. Using real people in shady ways in his fiction seems to be the sum total of his crimes."

"But you don't get killed for no reason, Archie. He must have done something."

"I suppose so. Do you want more tea?"

"Please. This is definitely turning into a two cup problem."

"Ha! Very good."

"We've been referencing Christie from the beginning. Perhaps Conan-Doyle will help us make more sense of it all."

When Archie returned with a pot of chamomile tea, Lilly shared her thoughts that the murder scene was set to resemble the book, but that in her opinion it was sloppily done and therefore a last minute decision.

"Unless the murderer was trying to make a point. Katherine, for example."

"You seem quite convinced of Katherine's culpability, Archie, even though she has an alibi."

"Not completely, but I still think she's our best bet. Barney could have been lying. Or he might have got the times wrong."

Lilly shook her head. She believed Barney, and she didn't think he'd been coerced by Katherine at all. With his marriage at risk, if his infidelity became public knowledge, he simply had too much to lose. He could have very easily kept quiet, but he didn't because he didn't want to be part of an injustice. She also doubted he'd mixed up the times.

"You obviously don't agree," Archie said. "So, what about Colin Kimble? I highly suspect he and Katherine are having an affair."

"Yes, I am too, but why kill Vincent? His and Katherine's relationship was long since over. Unless he felt he needed to defend his mistress for some reason?"

The two of them sighed. They were at a complete loss.

The carriage door opened, and they both looked up to find Kenneth Warren entering, followed by two detectives.

The police had arrived at last.

ANDREW WARREN APPROACHED and introduced the two detectives as Detective Inspector Chamberlain, a tall, thin man with sandy coloured hair and a beak nose. And a small petite woman with short dark hair and a pinched face, as Detective Constable Yarnell.

"They've just arrived," Kenneth said. "And when I explained you'd been looking into the murder, they wanted to speak with you."

Lilly and Archie rose and shook hands with both officers.

"I believe Mr Warren asked for your assistance?" DI Chamberlain said, frowning, and Archie and Lilly both nodded. "I understand why you felt compelled to say yes, but now you've contaminated the crime scene and spoken with not only the witnesses but obviously the killer as well. You've just made our job that much harder."

"We're sorry," Lilly said. "We were just trying to help."

"We've been told you've moved evidence from the crime scene. Is that right?" DC Yarnell said irritably, with an accent which Lilly found familiar but couldn't quite place.

Lilly nodded. "Yes, we found the murder weapon."

"Show us."

They all trooped back to the rear of the train, with Archie first showing them where and how he'd found the knife, before leading them to the far end of the main carriage. Archie unlocked the door and stood aside to let the police through.

Lilly explained what they'd found and where, including the book, matches, and glass. She explained about the Agatha Christie book and how the killer had made a sloppy attempt to copy the crime scene, along with her and Archie's thoughts on the reason why. Then showed them the knife in the bag.

"Please tell me neither of you touched the handle?" Yarnell said.

"No, of course we didn't. I picked it up using sugar tongs at the very end of the blade. Any fingerprints should still be intact."

Yarnell raised an eyebrow, an obviously well-practiced gesture, but said nothing.

Kenneth, Lilly and Archie stood by the door while the two detectives examined both the body and the scene. Taking photos on their phones and making notes in little black books. Eventually, DI Chamberlain turned to Kenneth and told him to seal the room. The crime scene technicians were on their way, apparently. He also took the key Archie had and slipped it into his own pocket.

"Right," he said, once they were back out in the corridor. "Tell me what happened with the passengers you've interviewed."

Yarnell looked at Lilly with contempt as she began to take notes. Obviously extremely disgruntled that mere amateurs had been allowed to get involved in the investigation.

Lilly turned to a page in her own notebook and began to explain in chronological order what she and Archie had found out so far.

"So, this Bobby Smith fought with the victim in a pub over Katherine Harp, then proceeded to form a relationship with her? And you caught them together in the bathroom, here?" the DC asked.

"That's right. Then there's Charlie, one of the train staff..." Lilly said, carrying on.

"Hot tea, right. Go on," the inspector said, as Yarnell scribbled furiously.

"Well, the Kimbles are next. Colin and Deborah. They know Katherine well and were introduced to Vincent through her."

"We heard Colin sabotaged Vincent's chances with some high level publishers at the conference today," Archie said. "And the love letter we found in Colin's bag seems to point to an affair between him and Katherine."

"Love letter?" DI Chamberlain said.

Lilly told him how they'd discovered it and what it had said. "It was definitely Katherine's handwriting, although both she and Colin denied it."

"Katherine was also convinced Vincent's book was about her, and her character would no doubt meet a vicious end. The manuscript was missing for a while, but then we found it in Katherine's bag. She denied knowing how it got there," Archie added, while Yarnell struggled to keep up with the notes.

"Is that all?"

"Not quite, Detective Inspector," Lilly said. "We spoke to an elderly lady called Milly. She's in the next carriage, so close to the crime scene. She told me Katherine came up to her at her table just before the murder. She also confirmed that all our other suspects had been in, or passed through, her carriage at some point not long before dinner was served. Which is when we ascertained Vincent was killed. However, another gentleman did come forward later and gave Katherine an alibi. Archie feels he may be either lying or coerced into telling lies for her. Personally, I think he's telling the truth."

DI Chamberlain nodded. "All right, thank you. Do you have anything else to add before we speak with these people ourselves?"

"Just one thing," Archie said. "I believe the cause of death was strangulation, and the stabbing came afterwards. Although why? I have no idea."

"Because of the amount of blood you mean? Yes, I noticed." He turned to his DC. "Got all that? Good. Let's start with Katherine Harp. As for you two," he turned back to Lilly and Archie. "Please return to your seats. We'll take it from here."

Chapter Fifteen

LILLY AND ARCHIE followed Kenneth Warren and the two detectives back through to their own carriage, noting that additional police officers had been called upon to guard either end of the carriage, relieving the train staff. Lilly was surprised to see Katherine once again sitting in her own seat, and surmised she must have returned while Lilly was asleep and Archie had gone in search of the coffees. The Kimbles were sitting side by side, with Bobby and Charlie together in another corner. All the suspects were in one place.

Once DI Chamberlain was satisfied, he and Yarnell left to begin re-interviewing the people she and Archie had already spoken to. Lilly desperately hoped they would find the person responsible for murdering Vincent soon, but realistically, they might have to wait until there was a positive match to any fingerprints on the knife. But surely they couldn't keep them on the train that long? The fingerprint analysis could take days.

After speaking briefly with one of the serving staff, who left to follow what orders he'd been given, Kenneth Warren joined them at their table.

"Better make yourselves comfortable, everyone," Colin Kimble shouted from the other end of the carriage. "We're going to be spending the night on the train."

Archie and Lilly exchanged glances, but remained silent. Colin was most probably right. Lilly felt frustrated that they hadn't managed to solve the case before the police arrived. But they'd done all they could.

Suddenly, the carriage door opened and the senior detective strode in and straight to Katherine's table.

"Katherine Harp," DI Chamberlain said. "You're under arrest for the murder of Vincent Wales."

"What?" she shrieked, all colour draining from her shocked face.

Lilly, too, was stunned. She was sure Barney had told her the truth. Had he retracted the information he'd given to her and, therefore, Katherine's alibi? And if so, for what possible reason? He'd really stuck his neck out to tell the truth in the first place, so what had changed in the last twenty minutes?

"But I have an alibi," Katherine said, as DI Chamberlain finished reading out her rights.

"He's retracted his statement and informed us he was lying," Yarnell said, with something akin to fury and disgust. Why would this be so personal to the detective? Lilly thought.

"Wait," Lilly said. "Why would he lie about that? It doesn't make sense." Then she stared at the Detective Constable, realising why her accent sounded familiar. Suddenly Lilly's words to Barney came back to haunt her. She'd told him a secret of this magnitude wouldn't be secret for long. His wife would find out, eventually. It would be better if he made a clean breast of it and told her himself rather than let her find out from a third party. She had just never expected for one moment it would be a police officer on the case who would recognise him. "You know Barney Waterson personally? You have the same Lincolnshire accent. Are you neighbours? You must know his wife too, then. Is she a friend?" Suddenly Lilly was livid. Barney was just protecting himself now, and obviously no longer cared about Katherine.

Detective Constable Yarnell fumed back at Lilly. "Yes, I am familiar with Barney Waterson. However, in no way whatsoever will that prevent me from doing my job properly and fairly. I hope you weren't suggesting otherwise, Miss Tweed?"

"He's worried about you telling his wife! Don't you see that? He's bound to change his tune now."

"Yes! Exactly!" Katherine said, grasping at the lifeline Lilly had thrown her and jumping out of her seat. "We were together at the time of the murder. I have an alibi."

"That's enough!" DI Chamberlain said, staring at each of them in turn, then looking back at Katherine. "It's not just the lack of an alibi, Miss Harp. You also had evidence taken from the crime scene in your luggage, as well as motive. According to several witnesses, the crime scene itself was made to look like part of the book you were offended over."

Katherine looked like she was going to scream. "I didn't put that blasted manuscript in my bag!"

Lilly knew with all the evidence stacked against her, Katherine couldn't possibly prove her innocence without an alibi. She and Archie had spent several hours combing over everything and the police were now about to arrest the wrong person over what? The fact a married man didn't want to admit to having an affair with a stranger on a train? She just couldn't keep quiet about it. "You're making a mistake," she said.

"I didn't do it," Katherine wailed, through anguished sobs.

The other passengers were staring open-mouthed at the chaos of the scene further down the train, when suddenly Colin got up and shouted.

"Stop! It was me. I killed him."

"OH, FOR HEAVEN'S sake," Archie said. "What now?"

What now, indeed? Lilly thought. She couldn't believe what she was hearing. She'd spent hours questioning this man, and throughout everything, he was adamant he was innocent. Why was he admitting to it now? Had he really done it, or was it yet another lie? And why?

The carriage grew silent as everyone stared at Colin, wondering what he would say next. But it was Deborah who leapt out of her seat and spoke.

"Colin, stop. What are you saying? You didn't do it!"

"I'm not going to let you arrest Katherine for something she didn't do," he said to the police, ignoring his wife's plea. "I killed Vincent. I strangled him to death. We had an argument at the conference. When we got back on the train, I went to speak with him and things escalated. I killed him."

The police were about to make another arrest, but Lilly had to be sure. While he knew a lot, she didn't think Colin knew everything about the murder. Only the person who had killed Vincent would know the answers to the questions she was about to ask. She stepped forward.

"You strangled him?" Lilly asked.

"Yes, I did."

"And then stabbed him?"

"Y... yes," he stammered.

"And you set the room to look like a scene from Murder on the Orient Express?"

"Yes, that's right."

"What did you do? Exactly?" Lilly said.

Colin blinked. "I've just told you."

"You haven't told us much, actually. What were the items you staged around the crime scene?"

The room was quiet for a moment as all eyes went from Lilly back to Colin.

"The matches and a glass. Um... the handkerchief and the, um, the pipe."

"And you opened the window too?"

"Yes. That's right. I opened the window."

Lilly shook her head. "You didn't, Colin. You're just repeating what you know from the book. The only items found were matches and a glass. There was no handkerchief or pipe. And the window wasn't opened. Why are you confessing if you didn't do it?"

"But I did!" Colin shouted. "I strangled him. Why won't you believe me?"

Suddenly Lilly realised that Colin was telling the truth. It was as plain as the nose on his face. Despite lying about the staging, she genuinely believed he had strangled Vincent Wales to death. But there was more to this story. She just hadn't found it yet. Before the police could move in and arrest him, she took a step closer.

"I believe you did strangle him, Colin. But you didn't stab him, did you? I know you didn't, so there's no point in lying anymore."

Colin looked down and shook his head. "No, but he was dead when I left."

"And you didn't stage the murder to look like the book either?"

"No, I didn't. But I am the one who killed him."

There was a strangled cry and Lilly turned to see Katherine collapse in her seat. She was pale but conscious. DC Yarnell moved forward and, taking a pair of rigid handcuffs from her belt, proceeded to cuff her.

"Is that really necessary?" Lilly asked.

"She's still a suspect, Miss Tweed," DI Chamberlain said.

"But Colin just confessed to strangling Vincent Wales."

"We heard him," the DI Replied, as Yarnell cuffed Colin and led him to a seat on his own. "But according to you, someone else stabbed him."

COLIN'S SUDDEN CONFESSION had thrown everything into confusion. The two detectives had left the carriage to meet the recently arrived technicians and take them to the crime scene. Bobby and Charlie had remained where they were, but sat in amazed silence. Deborah, who had moved to the seat opposite her husband, was murmuring in low tones through choking tears and Colin was shaking his head.

Archie leaned back in his seat and yawned. "I'm getting too old for this sort of thing. Goodness knows how long they expect us to remain here. I'm sorry our trip has turned so wretched, Lilly."

"It's hardly your fault, Archie. Up until returning to the train this evening, it really has been a lovely time." She opened her bag to get her phone to see if she had any missed messages and realised she still had Vincent's manuscript. She showed it to Archie.

"May as well read it, hadn't we?"

"Absolutely," Lilly agreed, having glanced and seen no messages on her phone.

"Considering we've been told, in no uncertain terms, to stay put, it's nice to have something to pass the time," Archie said, taking page one from Lilly's hand as she finished reading.

It was very well written, Lilly thought, although having named himself as the main detective, it smacked a little of narcissism. It was in the third chapter that Katherine's character was introduced as a failed romance writer who took great pleasure in ruining the lives of men by seducing then blackmailing them.

It was clear throughout the whole narrative that Vincent loosely based his characters on real people and then created the worst possible versions of them. And while Lilly wasn't really a fan of Katherine, Vincent's version was offensive in the extreme.

By the end of chapter four, the romance writer was found dead, after trying and failing to seduce Vincent's detective. Then the murder mystery was well under way. For the next couple of hours, while the real police were continuing their own investigation, Lilly and Archie continued to read Vincent's dramatic tale.

Over halfway through the book, they were surprised to find a number of other real-life people had made it into the book, including the Kimbles. They read on, unable to put down the story until they'd reached the dramatic conclusion; the character of Katherine had been sleeping with Colin's character for 'research,' as she herself was penning a romance story of a married man's affair. Eventually 'Colin' had killed her in order to keep her silent.

"Very interesting," Lilly said, turning back to the first page, where, as was his wont, Vincent had proclaimed it to be based on a true story.

"Isn't it?" Archie said, giving her a meaningful gaze.

Chapter Sixteen

S SHE DASHED down to the police officer guarding the carriage and asked him to get DI Chamberlain immediately, Lilly mentally berated herself for not thinking to read Vincent's manuscript sooner. She would have found all the answers she needed if only she had done.

Lilly returned to her seat while waiting for the detective. The other passengers were now fully aware that Lilly had made an important discovery and were badgering her to tell them. Especially Katherine, whose freedom was hanging in the balance.

"Do you know what happened?" Charlie asked.

Lilly nodded. "Yes, I do."

"I told you what happened," Colin shouted. "I strangled him."

"I know, but by your own admission, you didn't stab him and set up the scene, Colin. Someone else was responsible for all the dramatics."

The carriage was rife with speculation as to what she'd discovered, but Lilly remained silent and refused to be drawn into any conversation. She wouldn't say another word until the police returned.

Chamberlain and Yarnell arrived several minutes later, both looking annoyed at having been disturbed.

"I believe you have something to tell us, Miss Tweed," Chamberlain asked wearily, and Lilly saw Yarnell smirk.

"First, I'd like to apologise. I forgot I had Vincent's manuscript in my bag when Archie and I showed you all the evidence we had gathered."

DC Yarnell looked as though she were about to blow a fuse. "I should arrest you for withholding evidence, as well as interfering with a crime scene."

"Hang on, Yarnell," Chamberlain said, holding up a hand. "What have you found?" he asked Lilly.

"It was a genuine mistake that I kept it, but I now believe I know exactly what happened. Colin did strangle Vincent, killing him. But he's not responsible for anything else. You see, Katherine and Colin were having an affair, which explains the letter."

"She didn't write that letter, I told you," Colin said, but Lilly ignored him and continued.

"Somehow, Colin found out the entire plot of Vincent's novel. It's a murder mystery and all about Katherine. Just like the short stories on his blog, they are all based on a semblance of truth, which then morphs into the fantastical. Katherine admitted to me when I spoke to her that her promiscuous nature toward men, including those on this train, was research driven. Katherine," she said, turning toward the writer. "Are you currently writing a romance novel based on a married man having an affair?"

Katherine blushed. "Yes, I am."

"And did Vincent know about it?"

"He did. We talked about it at length while we were dating."

"And am I right in assuming you targeted Barney Waterson this evening because he is a married man?" Katherine nodded. "And that's also why you began an affair with Colin Kimble. You wanted the life experience being the other woman would give you to add realism to your stories. Whether it meant anything to Colin or was just a bit of fun, I don't know."

"So, what's your point?" Yarnell said.

"I'm getting there," Lilly assured her. "Colin found out the manuscript gave full and lurid details of the affair, and with it being blatantly obvious to anyone who read it which real life people the characters were based on, he had to try to stop any chances of it being published. That's why he went to the writer's conference. He bribed a number of people to arrange for Vincent's presentation time to be moved. His intention; to ensure there would be fewer people available and therefore interested in publishing the book, so reducing the chances of it being picked up. Unfortunately, the plan backfired, because he received a number of offers, anyway."

Chamberlain nodded. "So, Colin murdered Vincent to stop the unveiling of his affair to his wife and the public. With you so far. But who stabbed him, put the manuscript in Katherine's bag and staged the scene to look like the Christie novel?"

"I'm just coming to that," Lilly replied. "When Archie and I went to search everyone's bags, we were stopped by Deborah. Not because it was an invasion of privacy, but because that is where she hid the manuscript after she had stolen it."

THERE WERE SHOCKED gasps from everyone gathered, and they all turned to stare at Deborah. "What?" Colin cried. "No, that's rubbish. Deborah has nothing to do with this."

"She wouldn't let us search Colin's bag, so Archie and I left to go and ask Kenneth Warren to provide some support," Lilly continued. "And unfortunately, that's when Deborah was left alone in the carriage."

"That's right," Archie said, standing. "It's then that Deborah seized the moment and moved the manuscript from her husband's bag to Katherine's."

Lilly nodded. "Yes. Because although Colin didn't realise it, Deborah already knew about his affair with Katherine. And I would bet my eye teeth that she also knew Colin had strangled Vincent. She went to the rear carriage in search of her husband, but missed him. Instead, she found Vincent dead. She knew Colin must have been the one responsible and had done it to try to cover up the affair."

All eyes turned to Deborah, whose gaze was in her lap, but looked oddly composed.

"You're saying she stabbed the victim and staged the scene?" Yarnell asked Lilly. "But why?"

Lilly sighed. "Because Deborah loves her husband. And despite the affair, she didn't want him to go to prison. The crime scene was sloppy, and she knew he'd be caught sooner rather than later, so she decided to kill two birds with one stone. Protect her husband and get rid of his mistress."

"You were going to frame me?" Katherine shouted, launching herself from her seat with the intention of attacking Deborah. Luckily, DC Yarnell was fast and caught her before she was halfway down the aisle, frog marching her back to her seat and warning her to stay put.

"Yes, I'm afraid she was," Lilly said. "Almost everyone here was privy to your altercation with Vincent about the Agatha Christie book, Katherine, so Deborah set up the room as similar as she could to the novel, with the things she found at hand, in order to implicate you. She then used one of the knives she found among the catering supplies and stabbed Vincent twelve times. Finally, she searched, and found, the manuscript she knew would be close by, because she didn't want anyone to connect her husband to the murder."

"But she left a page behind," Archie added.

"And she did it on purpose," Lilly said. "I thought it was a mistake, but I was wrong. She wanted anyone investigating to see Katherine's thinly disguised name on the manuscript and so assume she was the guilty party. That, along with the other misdirection, meant it almost worked."

"Vincent was alive when I found him," Deborah said, speaking for the first time since Lilly had started her explanation. "I'm the one who killed him, not Colin."

"Oh, Deborah," Colin said. "He wasn't. I checked. You can't take the blame for his death," he said sadly as the realisation of what she had done to protect him, despite the affair, really began to sink in. "It's all my fault. You can't protect me anymore, darling."

DI Chamberlain nodded to Yarnell, who approached Katherine and, a little reluctantly, removed her handcuffs. She then approached the Kimbles.

"Until the post-mortem reveals categorically which came first, you're both under arrest for the murder of Vincent Wales," she said, slapping the handcuffs on Deborah and formerly reading them both their rights.

Lilly and Archie dropped into their seats, sighing deeply. Thank goodness that was over.

WITH THE KIMBLES officially under arrest and taken to a private holding area under the sharp gaze of a police constable, arrangements were made to begin the journey back to Plumpton Mallet.

The senior train traffic controller had eventually managed to get to the locomotive, and after a brief word with Kenneth Warren, along with Detective Inspector Chamberlain, agreed it had been necessary to pull the emergency brake. Work then began on resetting the brakes in each of the carriages so they could, at last, return home.

The rear carriage, where Vincent's body lay, was still a crime scene and had been uncoupled from the main train and hitched to an engine which had come from the Lakes. It would be taken back to a holding area to be processed properly.

Forty minutes after the arrest of Deborah and Colin, the wheels of The Lakes Express slowly began to turn, and the train chugged forward amidst a hiss of steam. Lilly could hear the cheers of the passengers in the other carriages and couldn't help but smile. She settled in her seat with the intention of doing the same as Archie, taking a nap, but was interrupted by Katherine Harp.

"I just want to say thanks for what you did. If it had been left up to the police, I'd still be under arrest."

"They would have found out the truth sooner or later."

"Yes, but I'd have been in handcuffs and dubbed a murderer for a lot longer than I was."

Lilly nodded. "You're welcome. I was furious when Barney rescinded his story, thinking at the time it was the only confirmation of your innocence. But, thanks to Vincent's manuscript, his alibi wasn't needed after all. Although, I believe he's just admitted he was with you to DC Yarnell?"

Katherine nodded. "She told him to tell his wife before news of the murder breaks."

"Good advice. I told him the same."

"I hate to say it, but I hope Vincent's book doesn't get published," Katherine said.

Privately, Lilly thought there was more chance than ever it would be. Now the author had been murdered under such dramatic circumstances. Tasteless as it was, it was a PR dream and in the hands of the right publishing house could very well hit number one on the bestseller lists. But that would be well into the future, once whoever now owned the manuscript was found.

Katherine thanked her again, then returned to her seat, where Bobby Smith was waiting for her, apologising for thinking she could have been a murderer. Finally, Lilly closed her eyes and let sleep take her.

Chapter Seventeen

BOTH LILLY AND Archie awoke slowly as the train eventually pulled into the station at Plumpton Mallet with a final screech of brakes and a hiss of steam. The two of them, along with the other passengers, had been warned they would be unable to disembark until the Kimbles had been escorted off the train to an awaiting police car. It was with mixed feelings that Lilly watched as they were taken through the stone archway of the station to the car park beyond.

"Well, what a ride that was!" Katherine exclaimed behind them as they stepped onto the platform. "I'll have to work that into one of my plots."

"I thought you wrote romance, not mysteries?" Archie said, pulling his jacket tighter against the wind.

"I was thinking it could have a bit of mystery on a train," she said. "Not murder, but there were certainly enough other stories going on to make a fantastic narrative."

Lilly had to agree with her. Between Vincent writing a book where Katherine met a nasty end and Katherine having illicit liaisons with half the train, she privately thought the romance writer had more than one novel's worth of interesting material to work with.

"That sounds interesting," she said politely.

"I wouldn't have pegged you as a fan, Lilly."

"I'm not really, but I'd certainly be willing to read a fictional account of the past several hours aboard that train."

"Well, just so you know, you will be depicted as the heroine who saved the woman from certain doom at the eleventh hour," she said, and Lilly laughed.

"Quite right," Archie said. "And what role will I play?"

"The heroine's love interest, of course," Katherine said, with a salacious wink.

"So," Archie said, putting his arm around Lilly's shoulder and guiding her to the rank of taxis parked outside. "When shall we take this lovely trip again? Kenneth Warren has kindly given us free tickets for whenever we want as a thank you."

"Oh, good grief, has he really? Well, that's very kind of him, but I think I'd rather keep off trains for the foreseeable future."

Archie pulled her in close and kissed the top of her head. "You and me both. What are you doing tomorrow, by the way?"

"Sunday? I've nothing planned, although I fully intend to have a long lie in. Why?"

"I happen to know a gorgeous country pub where we can get lunch, then take a leisurely walk around the reservoir, finishing with afternoon tea at a bijou hotel on the way back. How about it?"

"Now that sounds like my idea of a perfect Sunday, Archie," Lilly grinned.

"It's a date," he said. Stopping, he turned towards her and looked into her eyes. Then, moving in slowly, he kissed her deeply.

Lilly's response was instant. Her heart thumped and a tingling sensation swept up from her toes to the top of her head. Her last thought before closing her eyes and succumbing completely was; *what a perfect end to the day.*

If you enjoyed *Steeped in Murder*, the sixth book in the Tea & Sympathy series, please leave a review on Amazon. It really does help other readers find the books.

ABOUT THE AUTHOR

J. New is the author of *THE YELLOW COTTAGE VINTAGE MYSTERIES*, traditional English whodunits with a twist, set in the 1930's. Known for their clever humour as well as the interesting slant on the traditional murder mystery, they have all achieved Bestseller status on Amazon.

J. New also writes two contemporary cozy crime series:

THE TEA & SYMPATHY series featuring Lilly Tweed, former newspaper Agony Aunt now purveyor of fine teas at The Tea Emporium in the small English market town of Plumpton Mallet. Along with a regular cast of characters, including Earl Grey the shop cat.

THE FINCH & FISCHER series featuring mobile librarian Penny Finch and her rescue dog Fischer. Follow them as they dig up clues and sniff out red herrings in the six villages and hamlets that make up Hampsworthy Downs.

Jacquie was born in West Yorkshire, England. She studied art and design and after qualifying began work as an interior designer, moving onto fine art restoration and animal portraiture before making the decision to pursue her lifelong ambition to write. She now writes full time and lives with her partner of twenty-two years, her dog Oscar and twelve cats, all of whom she rescued.

If you would like to be kept up to date with new releases from J. New, you can sign up to her *Reader's Group* on her website www.jnewwrites.com where you will also receive a link to download the free e-book, *The Yellow Cottage Mystery*, the short-story prequel to The Yellow Cottage Vintage Mystery series.

9 798201 963828